Sea Stars Christmas

A STELLA MARE STORY

ANNIE M. BALLARD

DEVON STATION BOOKS

Sea Stars Christmas: A Stella Mare Story

Print ISBN: 978-1-7390170-3-3

Ebook ISBN: 978-1-7390170-2-6

Published by Devon Station Books, Fredericton, New Brunswick, Canada, E3A 2Z8

Book Cover by Claire Smith, BookSmith Design, Sydney, AU.

Editing by LZ Edits, Orlando, FL

Contents

Part I

Late November

Mackenzie yanked open the car door, barely noticing the cold metal on her hands. This place. Why did she still feel like an outsider? It didn't help to have local business owners griping about her. Well, to be fair, it was only a few, but they were loud.

Of course things felt unfamiliar when you start over, especially moving to Canada as she had, but she thought it would get better. Getting a job, a house and her dear boyfriend Declan hadn't given her a place in the wider community. People still made comments and she couldn't feel her roots. Sometimes it even felt like her life wasn't real. Right this minute, though, she felt entirely real and entirely stressed. Difficult meetings did that to her. She sat in her cold car, gripping the wheel as she stared into space. Was this new project even possible?

What a stupid idea.

Okay, it was her idea. That didn't mean it wasn't stupid. She'd dreamed it up, a holiday festival to highlight the little village she loved. She imagined visitors marveling at the architecture, the charming shops, and the excellent restaurants, all wrapped in Christmas cheer. Magda Allen, chair of the Village Marketing

Group, had run with the vision. Despite the naysayers, the group voted it in. Now it was up to Mackenzie to make it happen. In three weeks. Yes, a stupid idea.

A shiny Volvo swept up and Magda grandly gestured for her to put her car window down.

"Good job getting folks on board!" her sort-of boss said cheerily.

Mackenzie wrinkled her forehead. "Who? You heard the complaints. Those people don't like outsiders. Estelle and Josiah especially."

"Well, maybe," Magda admitted, "but most people really liked it. The hotel people, the chocolate guy. The restaurant folks."

"I guess." Mackenzie tended to remember the negative bits.

"Some people don't like change. Don't worry about it," Magda advised.

"When they complain about people from away it's hard not to take it personally," she said darkly.

"Estelle doesn't like anybody," Magda confirmed, "so it's not about you. Besides, they voted, and you got a green light."

"*We* did, not me. I'm an online marketer," she reminded her. "I don't do in-person, talk-to-people-I-don't-know stuff."

"You'll do fine," Magda enthused. "It's going to be fun and bring in business. The Sea Stars Festival will be the best festival ever in Stella Mare."

"Because it's the first," Mackenzie objected.

"And that's good enough," Magda said. "Keep connected. Let me know what I can do." Arm waving merrily out the window, she drove off.

Mackenzie could hardly fathom such confidence. If she did, then she could imagine Water Street full of lights and greenery, a parade with floats, bands, even Santa, and happy families watching. Maybe it wasn't such a reach.

It was even possible organizing this festival could help her get connected to this community. Hope bloomed in her chest, but then she recalled the grim faces of the naysayers and her heart sank again. She wasn't Magda, endlessly optimistic.

Remembering Josiah's glare didn't help, so she tried to shake it off while heading home. She wished she could unload her worries on Declan, but he was always busy. Teaching, writing, and, now, producing his play at the high school consumed his time. Besides, he was at work. She'd have to wait her turn for his attention.

"Mr. Kelly! Mr. Kelly!" The voice carried down the empty hallway.

Declan leaned out the door to see who was calling him. "Down here, Patrice." He returned to his position, standing over the printer and watching it spit out the pages of his play.

"Mrs. MacRae sent me to get it," Patrice said, out of breath. "Is it ready?"

Eyebrows raised, he said, "Chill. It's coming."

With a final sigh, the printer spat out the last page. He collected them and tapped them against the table. Their thickness against his palms was like holding hope, but he had no time to reflect. It was time to act, especially with Patrice standing there, waiting for Act Three.

He snapped the pages into a three-ring binder and closed it. Patrice had her hand out, but he clutched the notebook to his chest. "I'll walk down with you."

They entered the auditorium where kids were seated in the audience doing a read-through. Pat MacRae, in characteristic cardigan and sneakers and glasses on top of her head, delivered a warm smile from the front. "Patrice, you brought the playwright and the play. Mr. Kelly, good to see you."

Patrice scurried to her seat, and Declan walked toward his colleague. "Was that sarcasm? I've never heard you be sarcastic."

"Not a chance. I am happy to see you. I'm also very happy to see Act Three."

He laughed. "I know you've been waiting. Sorry about that."

"I'm just glad you both arrived. Now I can put you to work helping with the production." She turned to the chatting clusters of kids. "Take five, kids. Make it ten."

She turned to him. "Let's have it. The final version." She held out her hand.

"That sounds so, well, so final." He grinned. "I'd rather hand it over tomorrow."

"It is final. We need to get started." Her hand was still out.

"It's only one copy," he said.

"I'll copy it," she said. "One of the kids can do it. Dec, we need the script."

"I wanted Mackenzie to give it a look-over," he said, feeling silly.

"Declan," Pat said. "This is the final version for this production. No matter what."

He understood, of course. It was November and the end of the fall – show time – was looming.

He handed her the binder. "No more revisions. No matter what I think of in the middle of the night."

"The middle of the night is for sleeping. Quit worrying," Pat ordered. "We're all enjoying it so far. It's going to be fine."

"I hope so," he said. "But you always say things will be fine." He recalled being seventeen and consulting her as his school counsellor. "Even when I didn't dare apply to university."

"Have I been wrong yet?" she demanded.

He smiled and shook his head. "You're always right, but I still feel, I don't know, exposed."

"If you think having the kids read it is bad, just wait until the play opens," she said with a grin.

"You mean when the whole village gets to critique my work. Yeah, that'll be something." His stomach clenched slightly.

"We've got a few weeks," she said comfortably. "Lots to figure out. But at least now we have a completed script."

"Right." He tried to sound as confident as she did. "What else are we doing today?"

She looked at her watch. "We're almost finished for the day. We'll dig in again tomorrow. You and I can hatch a plan over coffee before classes start in the morning."

"Great. I'll see you in the teacher's room, then."

She nodded. "Give Mackenzie my best."

Climbing into his truck to head home, Declan was still unsettled. Maybe it was anticipatory jitters, or the new climax in the final act. He did know one thing for certain; he wanted Mackenzie to read this revision. Enough that he'd printed out another copy. Maybe there was still room for changes if she had suggestions.

Before driving out of the parking lot, he sent her a text. A reply appeared almost immediately.

I'd be honoured to read Act Three. I'm working right now, but I'll have time after dinner. Supper, that is.

Relaxing a little, he sent her a smiley in response to her joke. She was still getting used to local parlance; supper was the evening meal and dinner meant dinner out, or, for the older folks, the big midday meal. Folks from Stella Mare had supper. Away in Boston where Mackenzie grew up, people ate dinner.

Before he could drive off, another message appeared.

The strangest thing happened today. Guess who is organizing a holiday festival for the village? Yes, the most introverted anxious person you know.

She had added a smiley emoji.

And there's more.

The festival happens when your play is running.

He rubbed the back of his neck. He didn't know what she meant by a holiday festival, but it didn't sound too good, at least not for his partner. He prided himself on never getting too stressed. High school teachers needed to keep cool, so mostly he didn't get too worked up about stuff, especially stuff he couldn't control. But his neck was tight and his stomach jittery.

A festival and a play at the same time. Mackenzie would have her hands full. Actually, both of them would have full hands. He put the truck in gear.

Fifteen minutes later, the pickup crunched up the long gravel driveway. A trickle of smoke drifted from the new metal chimney and lamplight spilled across the frozen ruts of the driveway. The house was old, in a fair amount of disrepair, and looking at it always reminded him of all he wanted to accomplish. But tonight he was already rattled, so he focused on getting inside. Murphy, their big goldendoodle, greeted him at the back door. Hanging his jacket and pulling off boots in the mudroom, he heard music and felt the warmth of the sitting room almost before he pushed open the inner door. Murphy, never one to be left out, bounded to Mackenzie as she sat in front of her laptop.

"Hey."

"Hey, yourself. Welcome home." Her face lit up as she looked toward him. The crinkles beside her brown eyes warmed him as much as the smooth way she stood and reached for a hug. He held her carefully, then a little more tightly, inhaling her. What a pleasure to come home to her, his Mackenzie, this woman who almost literally appeared out of nowhere one early June day. He guessed this feeling was love. He knew he'd never felt so cared for, so warmly connected, with anyone else. Sunshine or storm, she was his person.

Right now, though, his belly still twisted with anxiety about his play. He dropped the script on the table to wrap her tightly in his arms. Even with a storm brewing in his gut, right here in this embrace there was peace. He didn't want to let go.

Mackenzie leaned into Declan, pressing her ear into his chest to hear his heartbeat. Reluctantly, she unwrapped her arms from his waist. "Well, that was the nicest thing to happen to me all day," she said, looking up at him. He looked serious.

"You're pretty sweet yourself," he said, releasing her. "Do you want to tell me about your festival?"

She sighed. "I'd rather not think about it right now. I've been trying to get things organized ever since I got home. I'll tell you at supper, okay?"

"Sure. In the meantime..." He nodded meaningfully toward the script.

"Is that it?"

"Yep." He gave it a one-finger tap. "Finally done, at least as done as I can let it be."

"What does Pat think?" Mackenzie asked. She appreciated the older woman's opinion in most things.

Declan glanced away. "I don't know yet. I just handed her the last act and left. I really wanted you to see it first," he said, making Mackenzie's heart squeeze.

"That's sweet," she said. "I'm honoured."

"If I hadn't taken so long, you would have been the first reader, but it got so late, I had to turn it in. It's the final version," he reminded. "Pat says absolutely no more changes unless they're driven by staging."

She looked at him with a little smile. "It must be hard to call it finished."

"Apparently. I've lollygagged enough, as some people might say."

She giggled. "Well, I'm delighted to read it. Can you rustle up something for us to eat while I read?"

"Sure." He gazed toward the kitchen. "What did you do all day, anyway?"

She narrowed her eyes. "I was working, remember? Even if I'm home, I'm working."

He grinned. "I know. Just poking at you. I don't expect you to have supper on the table for this poor working man."

"A good thing, too," she said, mock-fiercely. "But you're in luck. I happen to know that there's leftover rice and cold chicken."

"Ah, recycled leftovers. My favourite."

She watched him head to the kitchen, followed closely by the dog. She closed the laptop and picked up the script. She'd already read versions of the play, and she liked it. There was lots of local colour and fun stuff for kids to act out, and she was amazed Declan had dreamed it all up. She'd read his stories of fishing life, some already published, but knew he was working on a novel, alongside teaching. She didn't know how this play fit into his planned career as a novelist, but there it was, right on the table in front of her.

She scanned the first two acts to refresh her memory of characters, plot and scenes, then focused on Act Three. Gazing at the pages, she moved by memory from her straight chair to the squishy sofa, caught up in the story. Murphy, apparently bored in the kitchen, came in to clamber up beside her. The smell and sounds of food cooking were a pleasant backdrop to her reading. She was drawn into the tale of young people who lost loved ones to power of the tides, the storms and whirlpools, and the denizens of the deep waters of the Bay of Fundy.

"Hey, Declan, are there really man-eating whales in the Bay?" she called to the kitchen. He came to lean in the doorway, apron around his narrow hips, wooden spoon in hand.

"I took some poetic license there. I don't know if such a thing exists anywhere." He pondered a moment.

"No Moby Dick?"

He laughed. "Not locally. We do have right whales in the Bay. They're endangered, so their presence is monitored."

"Right whales? No left whales?" She snickered.

"Good joke," he said. "Whalers called them the 'right' whale, the correct one. No lefts! But we've got other whales, too. Haven't you gone whale-watching?"

She shook her head. "Another part of my education woefully lacking. Like I'd never heard of Glooscap, the giant who made the Bay."

"I wanted him for the villain, but it turns out, he's a benign presence who doesn't realize his own size and strength, according to the stories."

"He's just not a bad guy."

"Yeah. The whole plot would have been easier with somebody to hate."

Thoughtful, she said, "This story is more subtle than that."

"I wanted to avoid the superhero versus arch-enemy, but not get so complex it was beyond the kids. Plus, I wanted them to get to play dress-up."

She smiled and looked back at the pages in her lap. "Well, it looks like you've done it. I think they're going to have a lot of fun with this."

He came closer to sit beside her. "I hope so. I've never done a play before. Never even been in a play, so I suspect I've made a lot of mistakes."

"Pat will help," Mackenzie said comfortably.

"She has already," he said. "Hungry? Supper's ready."

"Thanks so much," Mackenzie said fervently. "It's great to share the cooking."

"As long as you're not picky," he agreed. They moved to the kitchen and put food on the table.

"We've talked about my stuff. Tell me about this festival thing." He looked up while taking a second helping.

"Well," she said, setting her fork on the table. "Today at the monthly meeting of the Village Marketing Group, Magda had this brilliant idea about a festival."

"Magda did?"

She scoffed. "Well, I might have mentioned it as a possibility. But Magda took it on. Even though it's just crazy to do it this year."

Declan's eyebrows lifted. "Like in less than a month?"

"Just like that," she agreed. "There was some pretty vocal opposition, but the vote passed. So yeah, I'm organizing this Sea Stars Festival." She grimaced.

Declan laughed. "You should see your face. But what a great way to get more connected to the community."

She let out a gusty sigh. "It's a hard way to meet people. If things don't work out, I could lose my regular job with the Marketing Group, not to mention make a fool of myself and them."

"What do you mean, 'if things don't work out'?"

"If it's not perfect. Like a Hallmark movie." She sighed.

"Perfect is an illusion," he said. "I prefer good enough."

She scoffed. This festival couldn't just be good enough. It had to be excellent. "It's a lot to pull off."

"You're good at organization."

"I'm willing to admit to that," she said with a little smile. "But organizing people requires talking to them. About things they might not like."

She looked up to see him smiling at her. "You're better at that than you realize," he said. "Just because you feel anxious doesn't mean you can't do it."

"That's a good thought. But people stress me out. I have to get business owners onboard for sales, a giveaway, a parade, and a window decorating contest."

He looked suitably impressed. "Sounds like a lot, but Magda's going to help you, right?"

She nodded. "I'll hold her to it. The first thing is to visit the village businesses to get engagement. Imagine me doing that."

He twinkled at her. "It does seem out of character, but I bet you'll end up enjoying it. People like you once you let them get to know you."

"Maybe. But the timing..."

"You don't have much time," he offered sympathetically.

"And you're going to be incredibly busy," she added. "It's all happening on the Saturday before Christmas."

"When everything happens in Stella Mare." He started to laugh, and she couldn't help it, she laughed, too.

Sobering, she said, "This festival is about the most challenging work experience I've ever had. I couldn't make it harder if I tried."

"It's great. It's going to be a great lead-up to Christmas. We'll make the most of it."

"I like your attitude, but I know it's going to land me in Stressville."

"I'll help," he promised. "As much as I can."

"Let's go have tea and talk about something else," she said. "I'm getting anxious already."

"I'll put the kettle on," he agreed. He went to the sink and she headed toward the living room. A moment later, he came in bearing tea. Steam rose from their mugs as he settled into the soft couch beside her.

"So....the play," he suggested.

"Yes, let's talk about that. I love how you make the place so important, almost like the Bay is a character."

He nodded and continued to meet her gaze. Encouraged, she continued. "I've noticed this, coming from Boston. This place by the bay has a peculiar influence, shaping people who live here. Like fishers. They leave and return, leave and return. Coming home means something different when you've been in danger out on the sea. This kind of life takes a certain courage."

"You see that in the play?"

"Absolutely. There's courage in being the ones left at home, too."

Declan narrowed his eyes. "I didn't put all that in the play."

She giggled. "Sure you did. Your hero character, he does it...comes and goes. Maybe you don't know how your own life experience shows up in your writing."

"Yeah," he said. "Maybe."

"It's your story, but it's not all made-up," she added. "You lived it."

"It's a fantasy, Mackenzie. Like a fairy tale."

She shook her head. "Sure. I get that. But there's more in there. My father was like one of your characters. He kept leaving Stella Mare, but he couldn't stay away. He returned, over and over. Then he died here." She gazed at her mug on the coffee table. Declan took her hand, and she looked up. "Your father, too. He didn't leave, but this place took his life."

Declan looked pensive. "He did leave. He spent a year in Toronto but came back to fish. Like everybody else, he worked hard. He died still working hard. That's the story here, or at least it was for generations."

"Yeah. Your play honours that but focused on the future, which makes sense for the kids."

"Thank you," he said seriously. "That's my hope."

"I wonder about how you'll stage some of these scenes, though. Like diving into water? It's going to take some imagination."

"Pat knows all about that stuff. I'll be her extra hands and eyes. Mostly I'm there to support the kids. They need it when they're doing something that challenges them."

"Everybody needs that," she said soberly. "It's not just kids. They're lucky to have Pat. And you."

"You know, Pat's one big reason I went to university. I didn't think I was smart enough, but she thought differently."

"And look at you now," Mackenzie said with a smile. "Teaching in your old high school."

"Yeah, well," he demurred, "it's not my endgame. It's temporary. Maybe this will be my last year of teaching. For sure, after the novel is done, I'll leave this job. Go somewhere."

She inhaled sharply. "I knew you planned to be a writer, but I thought you loved teaching." *And Stella Mare.*

He shrugged. "Teaching is a stopgap. I can't make a living writing short stories, so teaching English pays the bills."

"Of course," she agreed. "I thought you'd do both. Like you have been all this fall."

He shook his head lightly. "Nope. Never planned to settle into a career with a pension, you know. It's better for me to stay free and open."

She thought about their plans for the house. "I kind of thought we were putting down roots," she said slowly.

He tugged her closer. "I don't know about that," he said. "I think a writer needs to live lightly. Maybe what I can carry in my backpack, you know."

"I can see how teaching at the high school might interfere," she said. "You usually seem to enjoy your job, though."

"I do enjoy it," he agreed. "I love those kids, especially. But teaching isn't my chosen career, or my first love."

Deciding to leave the discussion about roots for later, Mackenzie leaned into him. "I thought I was your first love."

He wrapped his arms around her. "Nope. Just like I'm not yours. But you're my best love."

She squeezed him around his middle. "You're my best, too." But for the first time, his embrace left her chilled.

Monday - 19 days until Sea Stars

A week went by, but the following Monday morning, Mackenzie didn't waste any time heading into town. Last night's phone call from Magda weighed on her all night. She'd seen the moon travel across the sky from the bedroom window before sleep claimed her.

Magda had called after supper. "How many businesses have agreed to participate?" It was a reasonable question more than a week after Mackenzie had been tasked with festival planning.

"I've finished the logo and sent the banners to be printed," Mackenzie said with a pang of guilt.

"What about the businesses?" Magda persisted. "That's the critical factor. Who's left to contact?"

Mackenzie swallowed hard. "All of them."

There was a startled silence. "Mackenzie."

"I know," Mackenzie said, ashamed. "It's just that, you know, it's hard to just go out there and ask for something."

"You're asking them to participate in something that's going to bring them business. This is for everybody's good. It's not about getting handouts."

"I know," she agreed. "I've been avoiding this part. But I'll go, first thing in the morning. Face-to-face visits, like we agreed."

"You can do this," Magda encouraged. "Nobody will bite."

Mackenzie gave a hollow laugh. "Promise? I've just never been comfortable doing stuff like this."

"Well, it's good to stretch," Magda said. "I have faith in you."

As she got Murphy out of the car on Water Street, she thought about Magda. It was easy for her to talk to people. She was a real estate broker who had been in sales her entire career. Some people were good at it and some people just were not. Mackenzie was sure she was one of the latter. But she had a job to do and besides, she did want to feel at home in this village, so visit the businesses she would.

The cold, rainy December morning didn't help. Anxious butterflies danced in her belly, so she tried to breathe deeply, conscious of hearing the squawk of the sea gulls, seeing the mix of charming and rundown buildings, smelling salt in the cold air, feeling the uneven brick sidewalk underfoot. *I do love this little village.* She patted Murphy's curly head and the dog glanced up. Butterflies or not, she had to talk to strangers. Murphy's comforting calmness helped, but he couldn't do it for her.

She'd parked close to Dakin's Hardware. The grimy window displayed snow shovels, a couple of bags of ice melt, and an old, dusty plastic houseplant. "No Christmas spirit here, Murph," she muttered to the dog. "I don't think I'm ready for this." She remembered Charlie Dakin as one of the naysayers at the last Village Marketing Group meeting. Tall, heavyset, and grey, he seemed unfriendly, just like his window.

A pickup truck zipped by, spraying muddy water on her, her dog, and the sidewalk. Cringing, she watched the truck continue down the street, splattering another woman half a block away. The woman shouted, holding high a tray of take-out coffees. Her eyes met Mackenzie's, and they shared a rueful smile before the woman disappeared into a building.

Murphy shook reflexively, nose to tail, spraying her again. This time she laughed. "Yucky, Murphy! You'll need a bath." She shook off her arms, grateful for her raincoat. She gave the hardware store another glance, then walked across Market Square to where she'd seen the woman disappear. Charlie Dakin could wait. Instead, she'd try this art gallery, where that woman had disappeared. The sign overhead read Fishburne Gallery, Purveyors of Fine Art, and the big old mahogany door held a holly-bedecked wreath. At least there was a little holiday spirit here.

"Stay," she said before dropping Murphy's leash. He sank to the wet pavement and rested his head as she leaned on the mahogany door. "Good dog." She stepped into the gallery, hearing the jangle of an old bell above her head. *Here goes nothing.*

Closing the door on the cold, wet street brought her into warmth and light. Slipping her hood down, she turned slowly and took in the feeling of the place. Soft music, tall ceilings and carefully focused light – Mackenzie felt her shoulders drop as she walked through the gallery, around temporary walls to see each new work of art. She walked from one to another as if drawn by magic, while part of her mind noted the skill of the curator.

A large work, full of light and shadow, pulled her toward the back of the expansive space. As she walked toward it, another painting to her right seemed to call for her. Entranced, she drew closer to this primitive-looking painting of a seaside design. The more she looked at it, the more she could see.

"Hello."

Deeply immersed, she was startled by the greeting. She hadn't even noticed the woman now at her side. A tumble of dark curls and a warm smile welcomed her, but Mackenzie's shoulders tightened anyway.

"Sorry to startle you." the woman said. "Can I help you with anything?"

Mackenzie took a deep breath, willing her hands not to tremble. "Hi. I'm Mackenzie Brown."

"I'm Evie Madison. Is this your first visit?"

"Yes. You have some amazing work here."

Evie nodded. "Thank you. Some is local art, and others Leonard, the owner, brings from other places."

"Can you tell me anything about this one?" Mackenzie gestured to the bright painting that had caught her eye.

Evie said, "Sure," but she sounded anything but certain. Then she laughed. "That one's mine. I'm a little self-conscious about my own stuff. I do better talking about other people's art."

Disarmed, Mackenzie smiled. "I completely understand. But tell me. What is this?"

"This watercolour is a study of a hooked rug I found in the village, part of a project. The rugs are works of art, but aren't all carefully preserved, so the paintings are a way to fill out the design."

"Really," Mackenzie said. "Who made the rug?"

"Women in the village used to make everything, of course, and these rugs, or mats, were made of rags." Evie seemed to warm to this topic. "Most of them were functional but some were beautiful, and also amazing because of being made out of practically nothing."

"So you turned a local craft turned into a painting. And you're the painter."

"Well, yes, but I'm still learning about this kind of work. Are you interested in this piece?"

Abashed, Mackenzie replied, "I'm not really a customer. I'm here to ask you about the festival."

Just then, the mud-splashed woman emerged from some back area, calling, "Evie, we should get going."

"I'm talking to someone, Dorie," Evie said, then to Mackenzie, "That's my sister."

The sister arrived but stopped short when she saw Mackenzie. "It's you! I saw you out there," she said. "Did you get wet, too? And where's your – oh, wait."

She trotted to push open the front door. She leaned out to look, then called back, "What's his name? He's so handsome." She was beaming.

"There's a dog out there, right?" Evie asked. "Let me introduce you. Dorie, this is Mackenzie Brown. Mackenzie, my sister Dorie. She's a dog nut."

Dorie grinned. "I've been called worse. Can he come in? Evie?"

"I guess so," Evie agreed, but there was a question in her eyes.

Mackenzie brightened. "He's well behaved, and I can dry him off." She pulled a small towel out of her tote, while Dorie held the door wide for Murphy, who looked damp and delighted. Mackenzie squatted to take each of Murphy's paws in the towel. "This is Murphy. Say hi to Dorie and Evie," she instructed, and Murphy put out a paw to each of the sisters.

"Pretty charming," Evie conceded. Dorie squatted at goldendoodle eye level talking to Murphy and scratching his ears.

Mackenzie stood to rub Murphy's back with the towel and talk to Evie. "I'm here to see how the gallery plans to participate in the Sea Stars holiday festival."

"I heard about that," Evie said. "Leonard loves community events. I'm sure the gallery will help with whatever you want."

Mackenzie let out a relieved sigh. "Thank you."

"What's your angle? Do you work for Village Marketing?" Dorie asked from near the floor.

"Yes, usually just online, but somehow I got recruited to organize this festival."

"A festival sounds like fun," Evie commented. "What's going to happen?"

"Fun is what we're after," Mackenzie said. "Businesses will run sales, plus donate to a big giveaway basket. There'll be a parade, which needs sponsors, and there's a window decorating contest."

"All before Christmas," Evie said thoughtfully. "That's coming right up."

"Exactly," Mackenzie agreed. "We decided late, so we're playing by ear. We'll do what we can and make notes for next year's Sea Stars Festival."

"Sea Stars. That's pretty," said Dorie.

"I like it too. Stella Mare means that. Star of the sea. More or less."

"I never think about what it means," Dorie said. "It's just home."

"It's a cute name for a holiday festival," Evie agreed.

"Well, Nantucket has the Christmas Stroll, and Gagetown has Christmas in the Village, and Saint Jacques has their Harbour Lights Festival. We needed something that was distinctly about Stella Mare."

"Parade, sales, giveaway." Evie ticked them off on her fingers. Dorie was still communing with Murphy.

"We're building on a big weekend anyway. There's the high school play and St. James is having their holiday cookie and rummage sale and pie café."

Dorie giggled. "Pie café. Yum. I love the pie café."

Mackenzie grinned. "Coffee and homemade pie hosted by the church ladies. It'll bring in folks from elsewhere, we hope. The parade will be right here late in the afternoon, the play in the evening at the high school, and it all wraps up with a dance, the Sea Stars Ball."

"That's a lot. More than it sounded like at first," Evie said.

"Coconut cream. Pecan." Dorie's voice was dreamy. "I'm surprised Alice hasn't mentioned it. She makes the best pies in the world. And she belongs to St. James."

"Alice?" Mackenzie didn't know anyone named Alice.

"Alice Simmons is Chad's — my fiancé — Gram. We live at her place."

Things were falling into place in Mackenzie's mind. "You're Chad Simmons' girlfriend. You're the dog person, right?"

Evie laughed out loud. "That's exactly right. She's the dog person." She continued to chortle.

Dorie shot her sister a nasty look. "Yes, that's me. We run Best Friends Dog Sanctuary just north of town," she told Mackenzie. "Do you know Chad?"

"I do," Mackenzie said. "He's a friend of Declan's. Declan Kelly."

"Declan!" Evie exclaimed with pleasure. "He helped us move furniture last summer. He's lovely."

Dorie gave her an appraising look. "You're Declan's mystery girlfriend."

Mackenzie laughed. "There's not much mystery to me," she said. In fact, she was pretty sure everyone in town knew her story.

"Well, just because of Declan's reputation, you know," Dorie added matter-of-factly. "The guy who doesn't commit. I couldn't believe we didn't know you, somehow or other. This is a very small town."

Mackenzie gave a little laugh. "Well, I've only been here a year and a half, and I am from away." The words still pained her a little.

"Those magical words that tell you nothing," Dorie noted, "except you're not a third generation New Brunswicker."

Mackenzie giggled. "I'd never heard the expression until I came here. But I guess I'll always be from away in the minds of the locals."

"You can never get over it," Evie agreed. "My boyfriend is from North Carolina. Where are you from?"

"I'm from Massachusetts, but I've settled in. I even have my immigration papers and a job."

"And a very nice boyfriend," Dorie observed. "Chad really likes Dec. They've been biking all fall. Now they're talking about those fat bikes, but I don't think they're in our budget, not this year."

"Sounds silly. Fat bikes," Evie observed.

"They look a little silly, too, until you ride them," Mackenzie said. "They're great for winter riding."

"You ride, too?" Dorie asked.

"I try. I'm not as breakneck as those guys, and I have no desire to ride a mountain bike around in the winter, but it's a great way to get outdoors and give the dog some exercise." Murphy nudged her knee, and she patted his fuzzy head. "Okay, not just the dog. Me, too."

"You guys should come over," Dorie invited. "Come and see the dogs. Murphy might like that."

Mackenzie nodded. "That sounds fun." They exchanged numbers.

"Now, what should I ask Leonard for?" Evie asked. Before Mackenzie could answer, the bell over the door jangled. Mackenzie looked to see her friend Cassandra, tall, strong, and wrapped in a black wool cape, come through the door.

"Hey, everyone," Cassandra said. She shook back a tangle of pink and purple hair with a laugh. "Man, it is cold and nasty out there."

"Hi, Cassandra," Dorie called. "Nice to see you again."

"Is that Murphy? Hey, three of my favourite people and a great dog. Do you guys all know each other?" Cassandra scratched Murphy's ears.

"We do now," Dorie said. "We just figured out that Declan and Chad bike together."

"Right," Cassandra said. "Dec's my cousin."

Dorie scoffed. "No, really? Small town."

"Aren't we all fifth cousins or something?" Evie asked. "You only find these things out when you live in a little place. Except you, Cassandra, it's no surprise that you know everyone,"

Cassandra laughed. "Yeah, it's a benefit of being the only barista in town."

Mackenzie was busy connecting dots. "Is this the gallery where you work? When you're not making coffee at the Sunshine, I mean?"

Cassandra smiled, taking off her cape. "The coffee's only mediocre here, but this job has different benefits. I'm learning about curating art, and I hope I never stop. Leonard's been great."

"Speaking of Leonard," Evie said, "he left some notes on your desk."

"Okay, then, I'm on it," she said. "I'm on duty now, Evie. You and Dorie are going shopping, right?"

Evie frowned. "How do you always know everything?"

Dorie snickered. "I might have told her your salted caramel latté was a bribe."

"Yeah, and I'm not above using what I know," Cassandra said with a sly grin. "Watch out, Stella Mare. There are no secrets!"

"Cassandra, I'm working on the Sea Stars Festival plans. Can you talk to Sonny about it?" Mackenzie asked. "We need donations for a giveaway basket and there's a window decorating contest."

"Oh, sure. Sonny loves that stuff." The owner of the Sunshine Diner, coffee shop extraordinaire, often bent to Cassandra's will. "I'm up for the window decorating. It's a contest?"

Mackenzie nodded. "We'll find some judges or maybe the visitors will vote for their favourite downtown window. We haven't figured that out yet."

"What's the prize?" Dorie asked.

Mackenzie laughed. "We haven't figured that out, either."

"Bragging rights," Cassandra said. "Or a trophy. Reuse it next year."

"Good ideas." Mackenzie scribbled on her list. "I'll work on that."

"I have some great ideas for the windows. This will be fun," Cassandra said. "I can do the diner and the gallery."

Evie patted her on the shoulder. "Great. I'm delighted you want to volunteer, and I bet Leonard will be, too."

Mackenzie handed Evie some flyers. "Here's some information for you and Leonard, and for your customers."

Cassandra looked at them. "I'll take some back to Sonny, too, Mackenzie, so you don't have to stop by the Sunshine."

Mackenzie giggled. "What? I always stop by the Sunshine."

"You and everybody else in town," Cassandra said with a grin. "Okay, I'm off to work." She headed toward the back of the gallery.

Evie said. "We'll make sure the gallery has something good for the giveaway. Maybe a painting. It was great that you came by in person."

"Yeah, we finally got to meet you," Dorie added. "I'll give you a shout about dinner, but I need to check with Chad. We'll have fun."

Cheered, Mackenzie left the gallery. Maybe this task wasn't terrible after all.

Declan walked from desk to desk in the old classroom, where kids were more or less focused on their work. Some wrote longhand in journal notebooks while others tapped away at laptops or tablets. Chuck Thibodeau was slumped over his notebook, hair dangling in his face, untied hiking boots stuck out in the aisle.

"Trouble?" Declan asked in a whisper. Chuck looked up.

"No, it's okay," he said. "I'll get it."

Declan squinted at Chuck's empty page. "What are you going to get?" he asked. "There's nothing there."

Chuck shrugged and sniffed. "Something."

Declan leaned in. "What did that poem make you think about?"

"I dunno," Chuck said. "Nothing."

"What were you thinking about when I read it?"

Chuck gazed away. "Lunch." There was a snicker from a girl next to Declan, which he squelched with a glare.

"Yes?"

"Well, actually, fish for lunch, because of the sea in the story, I guess," Chuck expanded.

"Write about that. Just a reflection on how the poem influenced you."

Chuck looked dubious but picked up his pen.

"Mr. Kelly." A girl called out from the other side of the room. He picked his way through adolescent legs and feet toward her. "Yes, Ellen?"

"Did I do this right? I need an A on this assignment."

Declan barely suppressed a sigh. "Listen, guys, this is a reflection. You're writing about your responses to the poem. If you are writing about your own responses, then you are doing it right."

"But my grade..." she protested. "What about the grade?"

"This is an ungraded exercise."

"Ungraded! Why am I doing it?"

"Required," he added quickly, "but not graded. Reflect, people. Reflect." The bell rang, resulting in a burst of activity and noise as kids gathered books, backpacks, and friends to head out the door.

"See you at rehearsal, Mr. Kelly," another of the girls called out. "You, too, Chuck." A couple of other girls giggled. Chuck, gazing at the floor, slipped out the door, tugging his sweatshirt hood over his head.

Declan sighed as he watched them leave. Kids of all sorts, kids with friends, kids who were happier anywhere but school, kids who had no idea of the world outside little Stella Mare, and kids whose parents took them travelling every summer. Kids who didn't know what they had to offer, like Chuck, and kids who had to do everything right, like Ellen. He'd been more like Chuck, he decided, even though hoodies had not been allowed when he was in high school.

After he slid his laptop into his bag, he gazed for a long moment at his desk, lost in the past. He'd been an awkward kid, for sure, especially around girls. Then his gaze sharpened to focus on the picture tucked under the plexiglass; Mackenzie, squatting down in the wildflowers of their back field, an arm around Murphy. Well, at least he'd gotten better at talking to girls, if his current relationship was an indication.

Time to go to rehearsal and start the second half of his workday. Maybe there was still coffee in the staff room.

After Mackenzie's successful visits to the gallery, she tried the pottery studio and the bakery, with good results. Finally, she felt ready to take on Dakin's Hardware. Leaving Murphy out front, she straightened her shoulders and pushed open the door.

Tall shelves piled with housewares, small appliances, kitchen linens, and, further back, garden tools, hand tools, nails, screws, and plumbing supplies crowded the dark space. Looking down the aisle toward the distant counter, she stumbled over an intrusive snow shovel, barely avoiding a fall.

"Be careful!" The gruff voice came from the back of the store.

"Yes. Thanks." Reorienting herself and pushing the shovel out of the aisle, she headed toward the voice. A big-bellied, mutton-chop whiskered, and suspendered man watched her approach from under his John Deere hat. Charlie Dakin.

"Hi."

"Hiya. You okay? I might need to get those shovels out of the way." He gazed at her curiously. While not smiling, he seemed less gruff up close. "What can I do ya for?"

Tucking her clipboard under her arm, she stuck out her hand. "Hi, Mr. Dakin. I'm Mackenzie Brown."

He smiled a little and shook her hand. "I'm Charlie Dakin. Leave the mister out of it. I seen you at the Marketing Group meeting."

She smiled, a little unsteadily. "Hi, Charlie. Yes, we've met. I wanted to talk to you."

"Well, you got my attention. Probably didn't need to be quite so dramatic about it."

She flushed. "You mean tripping over the shovel? I'm clumsy at times."

"Happens to the best of us," he said. His eyes held a little twinkle. Maybe this wasn't going to be too bad.

"Do you have a few minutes to talk about the Sea Stars Festival?"

"Oh, that festival stuff. I didn't realize I was going to get a personal visit," he said. "Come have a seat. We can chat."

"My boyfriend and I have spent a lot of time in here," Mackenzie noted, looking around. "We're renovating an old house."

"That right?" Charlie asked, plunking himself on a chair and gesturing to another. "Who's your boyfriend?"

"Declan Kelly. Do you know him?"

Charlie chuckled. "I bin knowing that boy since he was a tot. You two are living out at the old Johnson place, right?"

"Yes. Not the oldest one, but I guess it's the old Johnson place."

"The oldest homestead prob'ly fell down for the first time in the 1800s. Nobody's going to be renovating that."

"Right. We're in the farmhouse. Much better than the old, old place."

He looked at her curiously. "You're Eric Johnson's girl. The other one."

She flushed again. She should be used to that by now. "Yes. Kathy's sister."

"Sorry about Eric," Charlie said.

Mackenzie swallowed hard. This was one of the things that made talking to people difficult; they knew her father better than she ever had. He'd died soon after she met him. She nodded, saying nothing.

Charlie looked at her kindly. "Eric was a good man. It's too bad what happened to him."

She gave another tight nod. Charlie, glancing at her sideways, continued without further comment on her family history. "I hope you're some hardy, out there in the country, in the cold. I got a good deal going on wood pellets right now."

She nodded. "I'll tell Declan. He put the stove in six weeks ago and it was none too soon. Cold comes early here."

"That it does," Charlie said comfortably. "Now what is this festival project?"

"You were at the meeting last week, I think. A village Christmas festival, to bring people in before winter shuts us down entirely." Mackenzie warmed to her subject. "Your business is year-round, of course, and winter is a big time for you, with all the things people need for winter. But a lot of village businesses depend on folks from out of town, so we're trying to make the village attractive for one more big weekend by inviting them to the Sea Stars Festival."

"Well, I told Magda it might be better for next year. It's too late to start now."

Mackenzie grimaced. "You're probably right, but as you know, the group voted to go for it. We'll make a bigger splash next year, if all goes well this year. It's kind of a trial run."

"Well, that sounds okay. What do you want from me?"

This whole interaction had been easier than she'd expected. "Well, a donation for our big giveaway basket would be great. If you have store specials, we'll advertise those for you. The parade floats need sponsors, and we'd love to have you participate in our window décor contest."

Charlie frowned. "Decorating the windows? Not something I thought of. But I can do a special on snow shovels or something. Salt for the driveway. Bird seed."

Mackenzie brightened. "Bird seed is great! Maybe we can have a craft stall where kids make bird feeders and they come to your store to buy seed." She scribbled on her pad.

Charlie gave a deliberate nod. "That might work."

"Pretty holiday windows might bring customers in." She tried to sound enticing.

He shrugged. "Maybe I can put up a few lights if I get some in stock. Some folks might like to get their decorations here, even though that dollar store place is cheaper."

She smiled broadly. "That would be wonderful. And, Charlie, don't take this wrong, but have you ever thought about playing Santa Claus?"

"What? Me?" He seemed startled. Mackenzie was surprised; he looked like a perfect Santa.

He slapped at his belly. "Nope, I'm no Santa. Heck, I don't even like kids. But you know who to ask?" He leaned closer. "You need to ask Billy Seymour. He's been Santa before. His beard's white, too, so no need for one of those fake ones."

Mackenzie was scribbling again. "Billy Seymour. Thank you. Where would I find him?"

Charlie snorted. "Just ask at the Sunshine. You'll find him."

She knew from experience that was likely to be true. "Okay, I will. Thanks, Charlie. If I come back in a couple of days, will you have details about the specials?"

"I can do that."

"And, Charlie..." she added, "I can bring you some lights to put up in your window."

He scoffed. "Get on with ya. I'm gonna put up my own lights. I can play along. I'll get my niece to do it; she likes decorating stuff."

"Wonderful. That's wonderful. I'll see you in a couple of days."

He walked her to the front door, where a lone customer was coming in.

She had ticked off almost all the downtown businesses on her list, with hasty notes about what each had agreed to do. At least she was meeting people. Heading home, her mind drifted. Charlie's mention of her father brought the past close again.

When she arrived a year and a half ago, she knew nobody, but she had hoped desperately to find Eric Johnson, the father she'd never known. She expected to be as anonymous as she was in Boston, where her last connection — her mother — had died. Instead, her appearance was discussed, speculated on, and a source of interest to many, much to her dismay. Finding Eric was easy because in this village, everybody knew everyone else and there were few secrets. But even Eric hadn't known about her until she arrived, looking for the only family she had left.

Now Eric was dead, but she had her sister Kathy, and she had Declan. They were reason enough to stay in Stella Mare. Their connections had formed readily, but did they have staying power? The sandy bayside soil didn't lend itself to deep roots, at least not for people 'from away.'

What would it feel like to be rooted? Her mother had left Maine, never to return, when she became pregnant at eighteen, choosing Boston for its anonymity and keeping herself and her daughter to herself. Mackenzie felt an emptiness in her heart that could only be longing. Longing to belong. Those words were the same. *Be longing, belong. I want to belong to people and to a place. I want Stella Mare to be my home, and I want Stella Mare to claim me.* But how to fill that empty longing?

Everybody had known her father, so they all thought they knew her, but not many knew her for real. She was easily pigeonholed as "the girl from the States" and "Eric's other girl." Feeling shy and out of place contributed to her sense of always being temporary. Now, though, she had a chance. Running a perfect Sea Stars Festival would cement her place in the village. She would be a committed member of the community, a person to count on. Not like her often-unreliable father. But like herself.

Things had worked out so far. When she arrived, she met Cassandra at the diner, of course, and Cassandra took her home to meet her mother, Pat MacRae. Pat and Cassandra helped her connect with Eric, Kathy, and Declan.

Dear Declan. Her eyes watered as she thought about how they came together. Neither had been looking for a partner. Declan really didn't have time for a relationship because he had his eye on his goals. He looked forward to spreading his wings beyond Stella Mare. And Mackenzie didn't expect to stay in Stella Mare, but she didn't have another plan. Declan was kind, and he felt dependable and solid, even in his commitment to his writing. She loved his clear-eyed compassion for his people in the fishing community. He'd known loss, as she had. Her life with Declan was full of treasures she'd never dared hope for, especially after her ill-fated first marriage.

Still, there were challenges.

Last June when her house-sitting gig ended, she'd moved into Eric's old farmhouse, and Declan moved in with her. That was great, especially when the house needed work she didn't know how to do. But they'd never really talked about what it meant. She had a house, he needed a place to live, they were dating, so it seemed obvious.

Once in it, she realized it had to mean something. They weren't just housemates. He'd tackled the renovations with gusto, and worked alongside her to create a home. She thought he wanted something lasting, just as she did. But when he talked about leaving teaching and Stella Mare to pursue his writing career, she felt uncertain. Untethered. Did they want the same things?

He was often hyper-focused on his work. She wanted him to have his writing, but also missed their together time. Perhaps she was naïve to think they could have it all. Couldn't they pursue their careers and have time to be a couple? Make a family?

He had never suggested anything about a family, though. His priorities were clearly stated: the first novel, and then the next novel. Maybe moving in together was simply a convenience for him.

She sighed. Being together wasn't always easy. She loved him for sure, but hated the feeling of being in a temporary relationship. They needed a conversation. Sometime when they weren't so busy.

She pulled her Corolla into the barn, leaving room for Declan's truck, and gathered her things from the car. Murphy trotted off at once to take care of business in the gathering dusk.

She pushed open the old kitchen door, flicking the lights, shucking her jacket and boots in one practised flow. Stepping into slippers, she leaned out the door and called for the dog. When he galumphed up, she let him in, latching the door firmly behind them.

The house was chilled and damp. Adjusting the thermostat on the almost-new pellet stove, she rubbed her arms, then found her sweater hanging in the mudroom.

Murphy rattled his dog bowl.

"Yeah, yeah," she said. "I'm hungry, too." She poured kibble into his bowl and refilled his water. She peered into the fridge.

She found Kathy's gift of leftover chicken stew in the refrigerator. Dumping it into a pot to warm on the back burner was gratifying. Instant dinner. Supper, she thought with an internal giggle.

Twenty minutes later, the stew simmered, the pellet stove pumped heat, and she shed her sweater while updating her files on the laptop. Steps at the back door made Murphy leap to his feet.

"Hey," Declan said, coming in. "Smells good in here." He bent to pat Murphy's head. Mackenzie got up to greet him, too.

"Are you going to pat me on the head?" she asked. "I could wag my tail if that's required."

He chuckled and reached to put a palm on her head, but then she giggled and slid into his arms. "I missed you."

"I missed you," he said, into her hair. Wrapping his arms tighter, he sighed. "Oh, it is so good to come home. You are so good to come home to."

She snuggled into the warm embrace, feeling tingling all over. "I can't believe what you still do to me," she murmured.

He laughed and held her at arm's length. "And what's that?"

"I'll tell you later," she said with a grin. "Right now, I have to stir the stew."

When they sat down to eat, Declan tucked into his chicken stew. "Man, that's good," he said with a sigh of satisfaction. "Lunch was a long time ago."

"Seven is pretty late to get home," Mackenzie noted. "Busy day?"

He groaned. "So busy. Not just classes and kids and Christmas play rehearsal, but administrative stuff that seems to go on forever."

"Hmm."

"I should warn you, today wasn't as late as things are going to get. It's going to get worse before it gets better." He looked a little worried.

She felt a little worried. "What do you mean, worse?"

"There's more work than time, especially with the play performance coming up. I'm often very late in December," he explained. "Even without a play."

"It does help if I know to expect it," Mackenzie said, "but it doesn't sound good. You're always busy already."

"Yeah. That's one reason we're perpetually in the middle of renovations."

"I'm not great with a hammer, Dec."

"I don't expect you to pick up my slack," he said. "I'm just not as available as I might like to be."

"Permanently."

"No, not permanently. December is just like that. It's my job and I shouldn't complain, but I'm complaining," he said with a laugh. "I'm looking forward to Christmas break."

She realized she was holding her breath. She let it out in a big sigh. "I am, too," she said. "This is our first Christmas in our home together, you know? I want it to be special."

"It's going to be special, just because it's first." He leaned back in his chair. "What do you remember about special Christmases?"

She shook her head. "No fair. I'm going to have think about that. What do you remember?"

He gazed at the ceiling. "Well, I remember before my dad died that we'd go to church, all dressed up, and there was music, and a lot of singing, and old ladies gave me candy that my mother said I shouldn't eat. They had a big tree with an angel on it, and I remember staring at that angel and wishing it could talk to me. Then after Dad and Uncle Mike were killed, I wondered if that angel talked to them. If I talked to the angel, maybe it could talk to Dad, tell him how things were for me and Mum. I loved that angel."

Mackenzie's eyes prickled. "Then you went to live with your aunt and uncle."

"A year later. After Mum died." He was silent for a moment. "Christmas with them was different. Nice different. Aunt Marge cooked up a storm starting in October, probably. They had Christmas dinner with the extended family, Aunt Marge's parents, and that crowd. That's where I connected with Jake," he added, looking up. "I probably wouldn't have met him otherwise. He's a distant cousin, not close."

Jake was her sister Kathy's husband. Mackenzie nodded. "I wondered how you and Jake were actually related."

"That's how. Complicated and distant."

"It was great for me, though, because you introduced me to Kathy." She recalled briefly that terrifying and wonderful event. "Your family memories sound lovely." She gazed at the table. "Mine were different, with just Mama and me. She was estranged from everyone, so it was just us."

"It sounds lonely." He was looking away, but she could feel his attention.

"No, not really. Or not always. When I was about eleven, our landlady invited us downstairs to her apartment for Christmas dinner. She had a white tree, full of artificial snow, you know, and had a rotating light shining on it in different colours."

"What did you think about that?"

"Oh, I wanted one, but Mama, you know, being from Maine, wouldn't hear of such a thing. No fake trees for her. She'd rather have no tree, she said, and that was what we had."

"No tree?" Declan said, aghast. "You didn't have a tree?"

"Nope. Too messy, too complicated, too expensive. We lived in a third-floor flat. Instead, we took an annual trip downtown to look at the tree in Boston Commons. You know, the one from Nova Scotia. I always pretended that it was our tree. I guess that was my first connection to the Maritimes."

"That's quite a story, isn't it?"

"Mine? Or Nova Scotia sending a tree to Boston?"

He laughed. "Okay, both. Halifax thanking Boston annually for help given in 1907. And your story about the Boston tree being your Christmas tree."

"It sounds a little sad, but it wasn't. It was just what we did for Christmas. That trip into Boston was an event. First, we'd visit Mama Mallard and her ducklings at the Public Garden. You know that children's book?"

He nodded. "I do because my grandmother made sure we all had Robert McCloskey's picture books. Did you see real ducks?"

"I'm sure there are real ducks, but we went to visit the sculptures. You can count on them not to fly south."

They shared a smile, and she continued. "Then we'd have a very proper, grown-up tea at the Taj Tea Room. Nothing quite like afternoon tea in Boston. That was a big girl Christmas treat. After dark, we'd go to see our tree. It was a special day for me, and I looked forward to it." Mackenzie's voice deepened, remembering. "Mama avoided relatives, and she didn't seem to have any friends, either, so we just kept to ourselves. I usually got one gift on Christmas day, but the big celebration was our holiday trip to Boston."

He reached for her hand. "Well, now we get to make our own traditions. Our house, our holiday. I want a tree."

She smiled. "I want a tree, too. Heaven knows there's a pile of them out there." She waved vaguely to the rear of the property. "We can find one any-where."

He looked at her curiously. "Did you never have a tree, even with Andrew?" Andrew was her former husband.

"We always went away for the holidays," she said, looking away. "Well, except one year when he wanted to host a holiday party for his work buddies, and he hired a decorator who did it all. But I don't really want to talk about that." *The only good thing that came from that marriage was Murphy, and he almost didn't happen.* She was glad Declan didn't pursue the point.

"You really don't have Christmas tree experience," he said. "We can't just grab one from the woods. Or we could, but it wouldn't be a nice one. Christmas trees are carefully shaped for years. We'll buy one. We'll support a local farmer that way, and sometimes tree sales also support charities."

"Oh, talking about charities reminds me," Mackenzie said, "I met Dorie Madison today."

Declan laughed. "Chad's girl. But how did you go from charities to Dorie?"

"Doesn't she run a dog hotel or something? For old dogs? I thought it was a charity."

"Dog sanctuary, and yes, it's a non-profit and they always need funding. Where did you run into her?"

"She was at the Fishburne Gallery. I was doing my rounds to drum up interest in the Sea Stars Festival," Mackenzie said with a grimace.

"You went door to door? You must be worn out," Declan said.

"I thought it would be terrible, but everyone was nice. Lovely. I wanted this job to help me meet more people in town."

"It's working. You met Dorie," Declan leaned his face on his hand. He looked tired.

"I met her sister Evie, too. She works at the gallery where Cassandra works."

"I was in school with Evie," Declan said absently. He yawned and stretched. "What can we do to make sure we both have a good Christmas? I want to have some fun, enjoy time off from school, and get outdoors. Ski, if there's snow. That's really it for me."

She considered. "I don't really know what I want, except we both want a tree."

Murphy pressed against her leg. "You, too?" she asked and laughed. "Okay, we three."

Declan smiled sleepily. "We'll have a tree."

"If we have a tree, maybe we could invite people for dinner."

"Doesn't Kathy do that? We went to her house last year."

Mackenzie nodded. "It was great to have a family Christmas dinner last year. I think I might like to take a turn, now that we have a house."

Declan scoffed, looking around. "Such as it is. Don't expect any big renos to happen in time for Christmas dinner."

"Right. If we have guests, they'll have to be forgiving."

"We can just hand out hard hats and tell everyone it's a construction site."

"That wouldn't be wrong." She smiled. "I'm going to get these dishes done. You probably have homework."

"Of course I do," he sighed. "Thanks for cleaning up. I know you cooked."

"Warmed up. It was no trouble." She leaned in for a kiss and then started clearing the table.

Declan rubbed his face with both hands. Tired, that's what he was, but there was no hope for it. He had to keep plugging at this novel, or his last three years of writing would go for nothing. Arching his back, he stretched his hands over his head, then returned to his laptop.

The words danced on the screen. Maybe sleep was a better option. He'd already spent two hours marking kids' papers and Mackenzie had gone to bed an hour ago. He gave the screen a regretful look, then closed the file. Tonight was not the night. Besides, it wasn't like he hadn't published anything. He had two short stories in a literary magazine, and there was the play. He gazed unseeing at the laptop screen.

Back awhile, a summer ago, he'd been working with Russ Johnson on his fishing boat, but it was mostly to hear the stories. Every adversity was met with a story and turned into another story, fodder for his novel. The old guys, the ones who didn't go out to fish anymore but sat around the docks drinking coffee, were the best sources of the old stories. When Cassandra introduced him to Mackenzie, he was struck by her story – an unknown connection to Stella Mare, and a missing father. Before long, he became part of the story, no longer an observer.

Everybody has a story. I just want to tell them. He'd been painstakingly putting together his novel, despite distractions. That summer, Mackenzie's story turned into the distraction of Mackenzie herself, her softness, her kindness, her concern about doing things right. By midwinter, he couldn't get enough of her. When she decided to move into the farmhouse, he was right there. The day he'd moved in, bringing a couch, a table, and a desk, she produced a bottle of champagne. "To new beginnings!" she'd said and he lifted his glass. It was the start of a story, but then real life asserted itself. The school year began and things changed. Teaching paid the bills, of course, but it also took time, lots of time. An old farmhouse took time and energy. He set aside the novel to make room for the play and the kids.

Oh, the kids. You'd think after ten years, he'd be immune to whatever teenagers brought, but it wasn't true. The drama of high school was full of delight, annoyance, and irritation, not necessarily in that order. He remembered being a teen: an awkward, gangly kid without a family, raised by his aunt and uncle, painfully quiet among the raucous boys from large families. His English teacher, Mrs. Fitz, had seen something in him everybody else missed. She had believed he was an observer and a writer, and when Pat MacRae corroborated it, he could believe it too.

He'd never been a loner, but for sure he hadn't been a leader. *Not my style,* he thought now with a tiny smile. So how did it happen that now he was the teacher? He got to be the one who looked inside kids to see what they didn't see themselves.

He sighed and closed the laptop. No more work tonight.

He filled the hopper on the pellet stove and turned down the temperature. Following Murphy into the night, he waited on the back door stoop while the dog did his evening rounds. An owl hooted. The moon shimmered over the tall spruces, crisp air holding a promise of snow. He yawned and the icy air filled his throat.

The cold was just starting to penetrate his wool sweater when the dog bounded back to the house, pushing past him into the kitchen. Declan closed and locked the door, flicked off the kitchen lights, and headed up to bed. This was his favourite moment of the day. Work was over, he was buttoning up his house to keep his family safe and when he got to bed, it would be warm and comfortably populated with his girl. What could be better?

He peered into the dusky room. Somehow, Murphy had beaten him up the stairs and already curled up on the floor at the foot of the bed. Declan knew sometime in the night, he'd clamber up to share with his people, but he started in his assigned position. He barely lifted his nose as Dec tiptoed by to get in bed.

When he slid between the covers, Mackenzie moved. "Hey," she murmured sleepily.

"Good night," he whispered back, kissing her cheek. He settled down under the duvet, tucking his pillow under his head just the way he liked it. This was the best. He gazed toward the lump that was Mackenzie, noting the gentle rise and fall of her breath. I am the luckiest, he thought. Before he could form another thought, he fell asleep.

Part II

Monday - 12 days until Sea Stars

It was Monday again, a whole week closer to the Festival, and Mackenzie's stomach was tight as soon as she woke. Pulling on sweats, she headed quietly down the stairs, followed by Murphy. After she let him out, she checked her calendar.

They'd had a great weekend; hiked in the woods, drank wine on Saturday night, and slept late on Sunday, carefully avoiding difficult conversations. It was easy to just enjoy things if you didn't worry about the future. Sometimes, though, the future was right there in your face. Staring at her calendar, she saw the Festival in red only twelve days away. How could she possibly pull this off?

She'd be home all morning, so she cranked up the thermostat, made the coffee, and queued up Maritime fiddle tunes. Declan bounded down the stairs looking for his travel mug and coffee and humming along to Natalie McMaster. Grabbing a muffin and his backpack, he leaned in for a kiss.

"You're running again," she noted.

"Always a little bit late these days," he agreed. "I'm going to be late tonight. Play practice."

A spike of irritation ran through her. "Don't you get a break? Pat's in charge."

"She's the director, but I'm her right hand," he said, "and besides, it's my play. You should come by. See how it's coming along."

"Is it different from the original script?"

He frowned. "Maybe. We're still doing revisions around staging. Stuff I'd never considered. The story's basically the same."

"Well, I'd like to come, but I don't think I can. Every time I think I've got this festival nailed down, something else happens. But thanks for the invitation."

"After the play, things will ease up. We'll be done with rehearsals and readings and all of that."

"Your play and my festival. Well, not mine, but my responsibility. We're both busy right through the weekend before Christmas."

"But then there's winter," he said with a grin. "Lots of free time."

"Yeah, but there'll be something else to keep you busy," she said, shocked her hear her own bitterness. "Papers to mark, poetry contests to judge, another book or play to write."

He stopped at the door and looked at her. "Mackenzie, that's my life. This is what I do."

She looked at the table, remorse competing with fear. "I know. I'm just feeling a little, I don't know, lonely." She looked up at his worried face. "I know you told me to expect this. It's just hard, but I can see you care how I feel. I'm okay, really. As you say, it's not going to be forever."

He gave her a quick grin and headed out the door. Maybe this was why he didn't have girlfriends. Everything seemed okay, until he pulled away into work. Her sigh was so loud she was afraid he might have heard it even in the driveway, but she stood up and gave herself a shake. If Declan didn't want to be with her, it was his job to say so. She wasn't going to make that decision for him.

Besides, he was busy. It wasn't his fault he had an interesting and demanding job, plus a true vocation as a writer.

I guess not everybody has a true vocation. Some days, just living life is enough challenge. I don't care about changing the world. I just want to find my place in it.

A place in Stella Mare and a place with Declan. But if that wasn't to be, well, she could manage. She was good at being on her own. She had lots of experience.

She peered out the window to see his truck turn onto the road at the end of their long driveway. Teaching high school, she thought for the thousandth time. Especially when his true love was writing, not teaching. How did he do it?

Well, her work wasn't doing itself. She pulled up the festival task list on her laptop. Some complete, some incomplete, some, well, some barely begun. The church events were managed internally. She'd nearly finished her visits with the downtown merchants. The parade – well, that had a long way to go. She felt both better and worse about the preparations.

This morning, she needed to get the merchants' sale and giveaway details. As she looked at her list, the Save Mart was conspicuously absent. She sighed gustily. She couldn't put it off any longer.

This most harrowing merchant visit was last, almost too late, with less than two weeks to go. Josiah Steeves and his wife, Estelle, had been overwhelmingly negative at the Marketing Group meeting. But the Save Mart was the only grocery store in town. She couldn't just ignore them, as much as she'd like to. She had to visit, and it had to be today. She wrote it on her list in all capital letters and turned to other things.

By noon, her breakfast muffin was a mere memory and her conscience was bothering her. She had to go to town, no matter how much she'd prefer to stay home. She called, "Murphy! Time to 'git her done', as they say around here."

Murphy trotted into the kitchen, ears up.

"You're always up for adventure," she said, patting his head. "We'll probably both find this afternoon very exciting."

Murphy sat regally tall in the back of her little Corolla as she drove into town, making her smile each time she glanced in the rear-view mirror. The road to town was icy in spots; Mackenzie watched carefully. She'd learned the hard way last winter about this local phenomenon called 'black ice.' Her little car still bore the scars from her brush against an oak tree. She had no desire to repeat the experience. But today was fine. The temperature was edging above freezing, but barely, even now well into the afternoon. Most days, it didn't get even that warm before the sun set early. Winter solstice is coming, she thought, and these short days won't last forever.

Driving down the now familiar country road into town, that thought seemed to ring in her head. Where else had she heard that recently? What else won't last forever? Oh, right, Declan's busyness. She scoffed internally. He was a lot busier than she'd realized when they were dating. Back then, it seemed like he had lots of time to spend with her. Even when they first moved into their house, he had been around a lot more.

To be fair, that had been summer vacation. Of course, he'd be home more. But still. She poked again at the lonely feeling, familiar and utterly unwelcome.

She sighed deeply and Murphy echoed the sound, making her smile. "It won't be forever, Murph. Declan said so."

Even if it is, Murph and I know how to be alone. We can be alone just fine. I only hate feeling lonely. I thought that was over.

Determined to put it behind her, she cranked up the music. She drove down the hill toward the intersection with Fish House Road. In an abrupt change of plan, she turned right toward the bay. Piloting the car over the rutted shell road, she approached the fishing docks, gulls and crows scattering in front of her vehicle.

The fish houses were spread along the waterfront of the commercial harbour, separate from the recreation and tourist docks. The big warehouse had been rebuilt after last year's fire, but the Johnson fish house was just an empty lot. She recalled coming down to comb through the burnt-out ruins in the weeks after the fire, hoping to find some of Eric's little wooden carvings. The only recognizable object was a charred cribbage board, which she had hauled out of the wreckage to keep.

Now, she pulled over on the sandy roadway and turned off the car. She cracked open the car window and listened to the sounds: rushing waters, complaining gulls, boats chugging into the harbour, heading for the long wharf.

Murphy whined a little. "Not today," she said. "We're going downtown." Still she waited, lingering in the past. The scent of woodsmoke from the old stove, the soft shuffling sound of a deck of cards, Eric's blue eyes peering at her face, his grudging respect for her cribbage game. His sparkling fiddle-playing. She wanted a father, someone she could rely on, cling to, after her year of loss, as she thought of it. The year included divorce, miscarriage and her mother's death. She had needed somebody to belong to. Instead, she took Eric by surprise, and besides, he'd had plenty of problems of his own. He hadn't been the kind of father you could cling to. They might have figured out how to be family, but he died before they even got to talk about it.

Of course that was sad, but I don't have to focus on it. Think about Kathy, instead, or Declan. I do have a family, not just the dog. But why does this festival mean so much? Do I need to show the entire village "Eric Johnson's other girl" could do something good? Approval-seeking, she thought. *Just like I used to do with Mama.*

The wind gusted around her car, startling her out of her reverie. Approval-seeking or not, she had a job to do. Starting the car, she headed back down the sandy roadway and turned right toward downtown. Of course, she wanted a successful festival. She didn't need to make it into some personal quest.

Water Street was holiday-ready. The beautifully wrought lampposts sported wreaths. The storefronts still carried that ragtag quality. Some were gorgeous spaces, of course, like the two art galleries and the Village Hall, a carefully restored stone building. The chocolate shop, two restaurants, and the wine store all boasted well-kept facades and attractive signage. But some of the other buildings were in disrepair. While the weathered wood was a beautiful detail, the buildings themselves were decaying.

Traffic was busy. Her slow progress down Water Street gave her ample time to consider possible improvements, but when a tiny parking spot opened in front of Dakin's Hardware, she expertly ferried her car in, briefly grateful for her mother's parallel parking lessons. She climbed out of the car, glanced toward the store, and was riveted.

The windows glowed. Fairy lights wrapped around dogwood twigs, a toy train circled a cotton-batting snow field, toy fishing boats floated on a mirror bay. Stacks of wrapped gifts glittered in the illumination, piled around an old wooden lobster trap lightly dusted with snow. The other window had a forest scene, with deer, a raccoon, and a snowy owl admiring a decorated spruce tree. Smiling widely, she headed into the store.

"Hello, there," said Charlie.

"Mr. Dakin, your windows look wonderful! You did a great job of getting the theme going."

"Call me Charlie, please," he reminded her. "Mr. Dakin's my dad."

"Charlie," she said happily. "They're so pretty!"

"My niece, like I said."

"She did a wonderful job," Mackenzie enthused.

"I'm still thinking about my giveaway for the festival," he said. "I was thinking a snow shovel but that's not likely to get anybody too excited. I found this. What do you think?" He showed her a picture.

"A bright red hot chocolate maker?"

"Nice, eh?"

"Very nice," she agreed. "I didn't know there was such a thing. I always use the kettle."

Charlie cocked his head. "Young lady, there's an appliance for anything anybody might want to do. Festive enough?"

"Charlie, that is perfect. Can you email me that picture? I'll put it in the advertising flyer. Everyone is going to want to take a chance on that."

"I'll do that. This Festival might be a good thing after all."

"You bet it is."

Was she hungry? She drove down Water Street. The Save Mart and the Sunshine Diner were on the same block. She thought about lunch, but then decided she was just procrastinating. Save Mart first. She could reward herself with lunch and one of Cassandra's coffees. But she couldn't bring herself to get out of the car. Instead, she parked and called Magda.

"Mackenzie! Nice to hear from you. How's it going?"

"I've got updates," she said. "Charlie Dakin's windows got the Christmas spirit! Even better, he's donating a hot chocolate machine for the giveaway."

"Great," Magda said. "With Charlie on board, everybody else will follow along."

"Really? I thought we already had pretty good uptake. The Chocolate Shoppe, the Sunshine, the two galleries are all participating."

"Right, yes," Magda said. "But Charlie's part of that old-school bunch. You know, the ones who don't think they have to market because everyone needs what they sell. Speaking of that, have you been to the Save Mart yet?"

Mackenzie's stomach tightened. "I've been avoiding it, but today is the day. I expect a hard sell."

"It might be. Josiah is not prone to generosity. If you like, I'll come with you."

Mackenzie's shoulders dropped. "Thank you. I was going to ask you."

"Josiah has trouble taking you seriously because you're from away." Mackenzie could hear Magda's smile.

Mackenzie sighed. "Right. Even though my father was a local guy, the locals cut me no slack."

"That's exactly right. Worse still, you're an American."

"Why is that worse?" Mackenzie asked, affronted.

Magda chuckled comfortably. "It isn't really worse, since most folks here have relatives over the border, or their immediate ancestors came across. Borders were pretty fluid for a long time. But you do have something. Let's call it a distinction."

"I have the dubious distinction of being from away and an American."

"It doesn't have to be dubious. Make something out of it."

Mackenzie frowned. "Like what?"

"Well, you already have. Remember your presentation about other places that had village Christmas festivals?"

"I certainly do."

"You got immediate credibility because you have been elsewhere and had other experience."

"I got immediate push-back because 'people from Stella Mare won't want to do that,' if you remember."

"People are doing it now, aren't they? Remember where that push-back came from?"

"Estelle. It was mostly Estelle."

"Who is married to Josiah."

"Ahhh. Okay. Yes, please come with me to the Save Mart. I need your credibility."

"We make a good team. When can you go?"

"Any time, really. I'm in town now. Parked in front of the Sunshine Diner."

"Come on over to the real estate office and we'll tackle him together."

Declan ate his lunch on the run. Heading to the little theatre during the school day was like running the gauntlet. He was determined to be on time for Pat MacRae's lunchtime meeting, but other people seemed equally determined to get in his way, literally and figuratively.

One of them was his vice principal, Aurora Smithers. She stopped in front of him in the corridor, calling his name and then leaning against the wall of lockers. She twirled a lock of long, blonde hair.

"Mr. Kelly," she said breathily, "how are things going with the play?"

He gestured with his pizza, chewing. "I'm on my way there now," he choked out around a mouthful. "Pat, uh, Mrs. MacRae can probably fill you in better than I can."

"We're so proud of our local playwright," she said, fluttering her hand. "It must feel so nice to have your work coming to life."

He considered. She made him think. "It does, thank you. I'm excited about it myself."

"My uncle is an agent. Have you done anything about publishing your play?"

"No, getting this up and running for the kids, that's my interest. He's a literary agent?"

She nodded. "He's interested in new talent. You're very talented, you know."

He shrugged and chewed. Where was this going?

"What do you think about celebrating your opening night?"

"We'll celebrate, but the party is after the show closes."

"I didn't mean with the students. I wondered if you'd be free for an adult beverage after opening night."

"That's a nice offer," he said. "My girlfriend Mackenzie and I would be delighted. What did you have in mind?"

She stood up straight. "I'll have to let you know. I have a meeting right now." She turned abruptly. Her heels click-click-clicked down the tile floor.

He bit into his pizza again and headed for the stairs. That was a little disturbing. She had input into his performance review. Maybe he'd just gotten a taste of what women went through. Or maybe she was just like most other women who were always coming up with ideas for him. Until Mackenzie. Finally, he had met a woman who had no demands, no designs on him. He practically had to talk her into letting him move in last summer. He was sure glad he'd persisted though.

When he got to the auditorium, the kids were milling around and talking in the front. A couple of the boys were pushing each other. Declan swallowed his last bite as he reached the stage. Immediately, he was bombarded with questions.

"Where's Mrs. MacRae?" a girl demanded. "She's supposed to listen to my lines, but she's not here."

"Hey, Mr. Kelly, can you look at this set design?"

"Mr. Kelly! Mr. Kelly!"

Total chaos and Pat nowhere in sight. He perched on the edge of the stage and took charge.

"We've only got thirty minutes, guys, so settle down."

"But Mr. Kelly, I need…"

"Take a seat, Patrice." Her theatrical sigh gusted across the space, but she threw herself into a seat, and the other students reluctantly followed.

"Who's got the clipboard?" Declan asked. "Okay, here you go. New sheet. If you have an issue, question or concern, write it down. Put your name on it. And your number too, so I can text if I have an answer. I can't take questions right now."

"But Mr. Kelly…"

He gave the group a stern look. Yep, this is me looking mean, he thought with an internal grin. What would Mackenzie think? "Time's short. Listen up. Chuck, you take notes, okay?"

Chuck, hair every which way and unkempt in his untied boots and layered shirts, looked surprised, then pleased. "Me? Uh, okay."

"So. Today we rehearse act one after school."

"Mr. Kelly?" A hand was raised.

"Is this about today, Ellie?"

"I have an orthodontist appointment. I can't rehearse today."

A collective sigh went up around the room. Ellie had a major role.

"Come on," said a girl, annoyed. "You knew what you signed on for. Somebody else could have had that part."

Ellie looked at Declan and shrugged.

"Understudy?"

"Yeah, I'm here," Ryann said. "I'll be there today."

"Okay, so, Ellie, we do act one again on Saturday morning. No scheduling conflicts, got it?" Declan used his teacher voice. "Got it?"

She nodded and subsided, whispering to the girl next to her, "I can't help if it I have to see my orthodontist. Not my fault."

Annoyance flared in his chest, but he counselled himself to ignore her comment. It was just kids being kids. "Okay, so act one folks are good for this afternoon. Act two tomorrow, act three on Friday and Saturday morning is a run-through, top to bottom, right? Nobody gets wild on Friday night because I expect you to bring your A game on Saturday."

"Does it have to be so early?" A whiny voice came from the back row. Derision flowed from the kids, and somebody threw a baseball hat at the complainer.

"Nine isn't all that early," Declan observed.

"Yeah," said Jimmy Smith. "When we fish in summer, we're out before four-thirty."

"Now there's an idea," Declan said. "Rehearse at four-thirty a.m. and you'll have all day to do homework."

A general outcry arose, and he chuckled along with the kids. "Nine a.m., full run through, no sets or costumes. But lights. Hey, technical...." He called up to the balcony. "You ready for a run through on Saturday a.m.?" The lights blinked twice. "Anything else?"

"Yeah. Where's Mrs. MacRae?" one of the girls asked.

Declan shrugged. "Busy. She'll be around. Now give me that clipboard. Chuck, do you have the notes? It's almost time to go to class."

Somebody handed him the list of items and Chuck's notes, and the students noisily prepared to leave, heading up the aisle toward the staircase.

Declan waved them off, then checked his watch before looking at the list of issues. No time now to do anything about any of them, he thought, but he took a picture of the list with his phone and sent it to Pat MacRae.

A ping sounded from the back of the auditorium where a door opened, spilling daylight in. "I'm so sorry, Dec," Pat said, fishing her phone from her pocket. "Student emergency, as usual."

Walking up the aisle toward her, he smiled. "That's an oxymoron, isn't it? But I get how emergencies are the regular job. Counsellor's life."

"Well, the job is like that, but hopefully not my whole life," she said, holding the door open for him. "I missed the whole meeting, and now you're off to class. It's a wonder any of this is getting done."

"The kids are doing well," Declan said. "Chuck took notes for me."

Pat laughed. "No kidding. Good for Chuck. And for you. I assumed you assigned it."

"He didn't volunteer, if that's what you mean. These activities help kids to stretch in all kinds of ways, not just artistic."

"That they do. Teachers and counsellors, too," she said wryly. "Let's plan to talk." They each headed off into their respective afternoons.

Mackenzie checked on Murphy snuggled into his fleecy blanket in the back of the Corolla. It was cold but the car got a little sun and he seemed happy to nap, which he'd be doing at home anyway. Seeing him cozy, she headed across the street where Magda, stylish in overcoat pantsuit, and impeccably waved hair, waited.

"Your building is so beautiful. An old bank, right?"

"It was a good renovation. Kept all the features but added the essentials."

"Amazing how you can make a wheelchair ramp look like it belongs with a period building like this."

"Not like the Save Mart," Magda said, and they turned together to look across the street. The grocery store was dingy, windows smeary, and the sign tilted off center. But it was busy. Ten people entered or left in the time it took Mackenzie and Magda to cross the street on the diagonal and entered through the automatic doors.

Bypassing the groceries, Magda went immediately to the office door beside the checkout lanes. She rapped authoritatively. "Josiah!"

The clerk at checkout barely gave them a glance. Mackenzie followed along, trying for invisibility. Magda pushed the door open.

"Hi, Estelle," Magda said, walking in, Mackenzie on her heels. "Is Josiah in? We need to talk to him."

Estelle frowned from her desk. "Magda," she said shortly.

"Nice to see you too," Magda said sweetly. "You remember Mackenzie, our consultant."

Estelle eyed her. "I do."

Magda went on. "We're here to talk to Josiah about the events for December."

Estelle's expression soured more. "You mean that Sea Stars Festival nonsense."

Mackenzie's stomach churned.

"Not nonsense if it brings more customers, is it?" Magda went on blithely. "Josiah? Are you here?" She strode to the inner door and peered through.

Mackenzie stayed close, not wanting to be left alone with Estelle.

"You might as well go in," Estelle said bitterly. "He'll be right back."

Magda raised her eyebrows at Mackenzie, and they sat in front of the desk in the untidy office. Mackenzie peered curiously at the bulletin board, layered with faded newspaper clippings. Here was Josiah, smiling as he threw out the first pitch at Little League, receiving thanks for his leadership of the St. Patrick's Parish mission project, then shaking hands with various men she couldn't recognize. She whispered to Magda, "He likes recognition, at least."

Magda looked at the clippings, too. "So he does," she said. "Let's keep that in mind."

A sudden beeping signalled a reversing truck outside the store, sending them both to their chairs. A door opened in the far wall and Josiah Steeves came in with a gust of cold air.

"Well, ladies," he said. "Look who came to visit."

"Josiah," Magda said, with a nod. "You remember Mackenzie Brown."

"I do, yes," he said, hanging up his jacket and moving toward his desk. "Eric Johnson's girl, right? The ba- the other one?"

Mackenzie flushed slightly, but said, "Yes. Eric was my father."

"Mm hm," Josiah said. "To what do I owe the pleasure?"

Magda elbowed Mackenzie.

"It's about the Sea Stars Festival," she said. "We'd like the Save Mart to participate, both in the giveaway and to sponsor a float for the parade."

"Hmm."

Magda gave her an encouraging smile and she plunged in. "We're planning a draw for the giveaway basket at the end of the parade. What will the Save Mart contribute?"

"Well, now, little lady, I've been in business for a lot of years and one thing I know is that you don't make no money by giving things away." He glowered. "What kind of parade are you talking about? What does all this have to do with Christmas, anyway?"

Mackenzie was still stuck on 'little lady' and couldn't find her voice. Magda slid in as if choreographed. "Josiah, you're right. Business is about buyers and sellers. It's also about community goodwill."

He frowned. "I have the goodwill of this community. This is the only grocery store in town. Need fosters goodwill, I'd say, Magda."

"You're right, of course, that the community needs the Save Mart. My boyfriend and I shop here every week," Mackenzie said, finally finding her voice. If he knew she was a customer, maybe he'd soften.

"Your boyfriend? You two living in sin? Hmph," Josiah said.

Mackenzie flushed further. "We're customers. Community members."

He looked at her critically. "Last I heard, you're from away. American."

Magda jumped in. "Josiah, Mackenzie has worked in marketing in different places. She's got experience in different types of markets."

"Hrmph. She don't know nuthin' about Stella Mare."

Magda's barely suppressed sigh was audible to Mackenzie. "She has things to offer we might not have considered. That's an asset."

"I want to learn," Mackenzie got out. "I also have some ideas."

"Your ideas are all about costing me money," he said, pulling out a ledger and pen. "I have work to do, ladies."

"It would only cost you a little to gain you a lot," Mackenzie said. She might as well go for broke. It couldn't get much worse.

He looked up.

She gulped, then pushed through. "Mr. Steeves, it sounds like Christmas is important to you. What if we focus on the meaning of Christmas? How about food for people in need?"

Magda probably was a good dance partner. She jumped in without missing a beat. "Save Mart leads the way in helping everyone have a merry Christmas," she said as if making an announcement.

He shook his head. "Let the churches do that. I don't think we have anything to discuss. You two can just go."

Mackenzie's heart sank. Magda pulled her chair closer to the desk.

"Josiah," Magda said, "just think about this. Do you want to be seen as a village benefactor, someone who cares about his community?"

"I do care about this community. This is my home, where me and Estelle raised our boys. Everybody knows I care."

"Imagine this," Magda urged. "Your business – Save Mart – is the face on the food drive. Save Mart gives the space to collect it, but people buy their contributions right here. It's a win in every direction."

"I think we're done here," he said curtly. "You two can go now."

"Josiah. It's not going to cost you a thing." Magda stood up. "If we walk out that door, Save Mart will miss an opportunity."

"I don't see any benefit to me or mine," he said heavily. "Or to our Lord, for that matter."

Mackenzie was thinking furiously. "Mr. Steeves. What about do unto others?" She heard a sharp intake of air from Magda but went on. "I don't know if you've ever been in the position of not having much for Christmas, but I have. When my mother was trying to raise me in Boston, all alone – "

"That no-good Eric Johnson," muttered Josiah.

"Well, he didn't know, but anyway, we had a couple of very nice holiday dinners because of community food drives. I remember a lady came to drop off a box of food, and my mother was so grateful she had tears in her eyes. I can tell you, when I was a child, it meant so much to have a holiday. To be like other people."

She was shaking. She wasn't sure where that memory had come from, but there it was. Silence filled the room.

"Fathers are supposed to look after their children," Josiah grumbled.

"He didn't know," Mackenzie repeated. "When he did find out, he tried. The house I live in now is thanks to my father."

"That right?" Josiah looked up under his brows. "Your mum was all alone, was she?"

"She was," Mackenzie agreed. "Getting help made a happy holiday."

"Let me think on this. Maybe we could collect the food here. It won't cost me nothing, like Magda said."

"I'm sure the churches will be grateful. Thank you, Josiah," Magda said, and grabbed Mackenzie by the arm. "We'll be in touch." She hustled the two of them toward the door.

"You, Mackenzie," Josiah called.

"Yes?" She turned back to look at him.

"You got any floats about Christmas? Real Christmas?"

"Floats," she said, looking at her clipboard. "Let me see what's in the line-up."

"We're still taking applications," Magda said. Mackenzie gave her a quick glance. Less than two weeks from the festival and they were taking applications? She shook her head and looked back at her sheet.

"This is what we've got. The high school is doing something about climate change, the scouts are celebrating families, the Legion is doing maple leaf stuff, and there's a float for Santa."

"I mean Christmas," he said grimly. "You need a float about the real reason for the season."

"You mean a religious float?" Magda asked sweetly. "Wouldn't that be something for the churches?"

He scoffed. "I might be interested in supporting that. Christmas is supposed to be about something more than sparkles and Santa."

"Actually," Mackenzie said, "I did have an inquiry from the Sunday school at the United Church. Maybe they'd like your help," she offered. "Can I tell them to get in touch with you?"

"Well, that might be okay," he allowed. "I'm not giving anything away to no tourists, though."

"We've established that," Mackenzie said. "You'll be the leader of the food drive, collecting the food here at the store, and you'll help the United Church with their float. Those are great contributions." Her smile felt genuine and warm.

Magda smiled, too. "Thank you, Josiah. This is going to be a wonderful event for Stella Mare, and I'm so glad we're all able to work together."

Josiah nearly smiled back as he accompanied them to the door to the outer office. "You two have a good day, now," he said as Magda opened the door. Estelle, her face twisted as if from a bitter taste, glared at them from the desk.

"What did you agree to?" she asked.

"Oh, you never mind," Josiah said with an airy wave. "Nothing too big. It's all for Christmas, anyhow." He closed himself in the inner office.

Mackenzie was relieved to be leaving, but Estelle had a parting shot.

"You there." Mackenzie stopped and slowly turned around.

"Me?"

Estelle jerked her chin, indicating Mackenzie should come closer. Mackenzie, stiff as a board but curious, approached. "Christmas is hard on single mums. On widows, too. You know," Estelle said, barely above a whisper.

"Uh, yes?" Mackenzie was uncertain.

The older woman pulled a faded flyer from a desk drawer. "Here, you take this. You need to know about this."

"Thanks," Mackenzie whispered back, gazing at the paper that appeared in her hand.

Estelle suddenly got a lot louder. "Now you two go on, with your high-fa-lutin' festivals and all that nonsense." She jerked her chin toward the door, and a shadow passed over her face.

"We're going, Estelle," Magda said. "No need to shout."

She led the way through the store and into the wintry sunshine. Hurrying in tandem down the street, they made it about half a block before Mackenzie's sideways glance at Magda caused them both to burst into laughter.

"That Estelle." Magda let out a gusty sigh.

"So confusing! If looks could kill, we'd be dead on the floor," Mackenzie spluttered through her giggles. "And yet there's something more." Mackenzie held up the faded flyer. Even squinting, she couldn't make out the print. "Can you read this?"

Magda squinted too. "Seafaring something or other." She shrugged. "No idea. I wonder why she gave it to you."

"I'm sure there was a reason," Mackenzie said, "but if I can't read it, I can't figure it out. Seafaring what?" She peered more closely. "Sea Widows and Orphans. That's all, though. I can't make it out." Looking up at Magda, she asked, "Is that a charity or something?"

Magda shrugged again. "I never heard of it. I'm not sure it's important. Estelle and Josiah are quite a pair. I guess if I were married to Josiah, I might be miserable, too."

"She's unhappy. That's why she's difficult. I've known people like that." Mackenzie recalled her mother, whose unhappiness had made life small, sad, and lonely for them both.

"I suppose she could be," Magda conceded. "I just figure she's a mean old witch. Josiah, too, but you did a great job of talking his talk."

"That was all you," Mackenzie admitted. "He threw me off with that crack about not being married."

"We did very well," Magda said. "We're a good team."

Mackenzie touched her sleeve. "I am so glad you were there. Thank you."

"Happy to help you out, little lady," Magda said, and they were overcome with giggles once again.

"Lunch? Coffee?" Mackenzie suggested. "I'd like you to see my checklist. Now I'm starving."

"I never say no to coffee," Magda agreed. "Besides, I want to see what you've got."

They headed down Water Street to the Sunshine Diner. Mackenzie, thinking aloud, said, "We didn't plan to have a food drive, but now we're having one."

"Well, we started late, didn't set limits, and consequently we keep adding on. Your food drive idea allows Josiah to participate on his own terms. It's perfect for him."

"It's a racket. Josiah wins no matter what. He gets to look benevolent, and his sales will go up."

"It's okay," Magda said. "He's doing more than anybody expected, including him. He'll feel good about it, especially when he lands in the spotlight. Next year he'll be the first to volunteer."

"I hope his good feeling spills over to Estelle. I feel kind of sorry for her. But she's also scary."

Magda harrumphed. "You be sorry for her. She's just a thorn in my side, trying to block any idea I have for this village." She pulled open the heavy door to the diner. "Mm, smell the coffee." They entered the warm, steamy café and found a booth.

Shrugging out of her winter coat, Mackenzie settled into the comfortable familiarity of the Sunshine. "I love this place. It's where I met my first friend in Stella Mare. Here she comes now."

Cassandra arrived, smile in place. "Hey, Mackenzie, Magda. You guys doing festival work?"

"We are! And lunch, for me at least," Mackenzie said. "BLT and an Americano, please. Do you have any of Uncle Ray's cinnamon rolls? I feel like celebrating."

Cassandra grinned at them. "I must have had an intuition. I stashed a couple out back, and I bet they have your name on them. Coffee, Magda?"

"The usual, thanks," Magda confirmed.

"Can you sit for a bit?" Mackenzie asked. Turning to Magda, she added, "Cassandra's been helping me with ideas."

"Let me get started on this," Cassandra said, waving their order, "and then I'll see if I can take a break." She headed for the kitchen.

"I met Declan here," Mackenzie said dreamily. "Cassandra introduced us."

"For somebody from away, you've got some rich memories of Stella Mare," Magda observed.

"Yeah, I guess so."

"I'm from away, too, only I'm from PEI."

"From Prince Edward Island? I haven't been there yet."

"Oh, you'll have to go. It's the most beautiful place in Canada," Magda said fondly.

"I didn't know anyone ever left PEI," Mackenzie said with a grin. "I thought people only went home to the Island."

"That's what they tell you, but you've got to go away, if you ever want to return."

Mackenzie giggled. "That makes sense."

Cassandra put their coffee on the table and headed off to seat a group of customers. The steam rose, fogging the window. Mackenzie sipped appreciatively.

"Hot coffee on a cold day is perfect," Magda noted. "We've got Josiah taken care of. What else is there?"

Mackenzie smiled. "The rest of it might be do-able now that I'm less worried about Josiah and Estelle. But I'm still unsure about the parade. I don't know what I'm doing there."

"The parade might be the best part," Magda said. "It's a way to focus the attention of the visitors on the downtown. Families will bring their children to see Santa, and everyone will enjoy the floats."

"I'm not sure of the timing. The parade needs to end at twilight to maximize the Christmas lights. But we'll lose the little kids to bedtime if we start too late."

"Don't forget where you are," Magda warned. "This time of year, it's full dark by five. We could start the parade at four p.m., and folks will be ready for dinner by the end."

"The restaurants will be ready, and three of them have mobile kitchens they'll set up in Market Square. It's going to be perfect." Mackenzie felt a spurt of satisfaction at the thought.

"We don't need perfect. But it does sound great to have food right there where everybody lands at the end of the parade." Magda leaned back. "Who's handling the parade? The line-up and all that?"

Mackenzie looked up from her scribbling. "I just figured they'd work it out themselves," she said. "Is that naïve?"

Magda laughed. "People require direction. Maybe Kevin Ellison would help out."

"Kevin?" Mackenzie asked, writing again. "How do I find him?"

Magda looked at her watch. "I've got to go. Text me for Kevin's info." She slipped out of the booth, pulling on her coat. "What else?"

Mackenzie shook her head. "We're good. I'll finish my draft schedule and the flyer, and send them to the committee for approval."

Cassandra set Mackenzie's food in front of her, then sat herself, fanning her face with her apron. "Committee and approval are two words that should never appear in the same sentence."

"She's right," Magda agreed. "Don't wait for approval. Send them out as information items. Time is short."

Mackenzie was unconvinced. "I don't want to be in charge. I need back-up. What if Josiah decides he doesn't like my decisions?"

"I guess that could happen," Magda said. "Okay, I'll be your backup. You can run stuff by me before you send it out, but we're not going to try to do this democratically. You've been hired to do a job, and you get to do it your way."

Mackenzie let out a shocked laugh. "My way? I don't even know what that is."

"It'll be fine," Magda said, buttoning her coat. "It might not be everything everybody wants this year, but we're learning. Good work."

Mackenzie watched her wave as she went out the big front door. Cassandra turned to her. "Are you having any fun?"

Mackenzie smiled ruefully. "Well, I liked meeting Dorie and Evie. Charlie Dakin has turned out to be nice. But no, it isn't fun. I want it to be perfect, but we're so far off I don't know how to get there. Too many moving parts and too many loose ends. I might be too introverted for this job."

"You used to have trouble talking to strangers, but there aren't that many strangers in Stella Mare. The festival will be fun for visitors, and the committee is lucky to have you."

"I'm lucky to have you," Mackenzie threw back. "You're so practical."

"Thanks."

A moment passed, then Cassandra said, "The festival's a great start to Christmas. Get a little Sea Stars spirit."

"How do we make that happen?" Mackenzie asked, hopeful. "I'm not sure I've ever had Christmas spirit."

"Really?" Cassandra frowned. "It's a nice feeling when it comes but it's unpredictable. Most times, I'm just doing my regular life, you know, then something happens, zap, and it hits me."

"Something like what?" Mackenzie was curious.

"It could just be snow," she said. "Or somebody being, I don't know, uncharacteristically nice. When people feel kindly toward each other, then they act more kindly, and then I feel it."

"It's not the lights and decorations?"

"Those are mostly reminders. Sometimes Christmas just feels like extra work, but then something happens, it's like you flipped a switch, and everything is suddenly worth it. Beautiful, even if yesterday it was just plain old everyday life."

"Yeah. That's the feeling we're after. Turning plain old everyday Stella Mare into a magical Sea Star Festival, where everybody feels good."

"That's a tall order, but a good aspiration," Cassandra said. She paused. "Since we don't know how to flip the spirit switch, we can work on the decorations."

"It's a concrete place to start, and hope the spirit arrives." Mackenzie smiled at her friend.

"Let the season do its magic. There is something about getting together before we all hunker down for the winter," Cassandra mused. "Music, good food, pretty lights, and an opportunity to be a good neighbour. They help us face down a long cold winter."

"I had a picture book when I was small," Mackenzie remembered, "about a field mouse who got in trouble because he didn't gather food for the winter. Instead, he gathered images and stories. When winter came, the other mice loved the memories he had saved. My mother didn't like it. She thought he was lazy, but I loved that book. I might still have it somewhere."

"Maybe that's what art is for. But for right now, work is calling. Let me know what I can do to help, okay?"

"Thanks, Cassandra. You're doing lots, you know, with windows here and at the gallery, and you're helping the high school kids with a float, did I hear that right?"

"Yeah, my mother recruited me for that one. But I'm still happy to help you out."

Mackenzie nodded her thanks. "Good. I'll be in touch."

Wednesday - 10 days until Sea Stars

Mackenzie looked at her phone with regret. Dorie had texted with an invitation, but it just couldn't work. Declan most certainly was not available on Friday evening. Fridays were always late because of the play, she thought, trying not to feel bitter. She forwarded the invitation anyway. She didn't want to speak for Declan.

A ping alerted her to Dec's expected answer. Friday was out unless it was late, but he had early rehearsal on Saturday so late wouldn't work anyway.

She sighed, but replied with a thumbs up, then replied to Dorie.

Mackenzie: *Declan's got to work on the play but thank you. That's very kind.*

Dorie: *Working on Friday night? Obsessed much?*

Mackenzie, faintly offended on Declan's behalf: *Committed, I think.*

Dorie: *Yeah, that was uncalled for. Chad and I work odd hours too. Hey, do you want to get a coffee? Or come out to the dog sanctuary? I make coffee here. It's not the Sunshine but it has caffeine.*

Mackenzie's heart warmed. Yes, she did want to visit with Dorie. Or somebody. Right now, being alone at the farmhouse was unappealing. They planned for late afternoon.

Declan peered into the empty staff room. School was over, staff were gone, and he had an hour before play practice to catch up on a few things. Spying the coffee maker, he poured the dregs from the carafe into his mug and stuck it in the microwave. He inspected the inside of the refrigerator, only then recalling he'd left home without making his lunch. Instead, he pulled a protein bar from his back pocket. That would do. It would fill him up enough to focus.

The coffee was wonderfully hot but tasted burnt. He sat at the wobbly table to make his calls to parents, chewing and sipping between conversations. This might be his least favourite part of being a teacher. It was never fun to inform a parent of a kid's struggles in class, but it was necessary. On occasion he'd been able to create a working alliance with parents that actually helped a kid. Maybe today would be like that.

The first three numbers accessed voicemail, so he left his number and a request for a call. Four other parents answered, but most were defensive and oblivious.

"Mrs. Ellis, she hasn't turned in any work since Halloween. I've emailed you weekly, but since I didn't hear from you, I'm calling to update you." He covered a yawn as he listened to a litany of explanation. "Thank you for your attention to this," he said when he could get a word in. "I just wanted to give you some warning, so you won't be surprised when grades come out next month. Unless there is substantial change, she'll have to retake the semester."

He yawned again, larger this time. "Yes, you can talk to the principal. Be my guest."

So many excuses, when the kid just needs somebody who thinks schoolwork matters. I was a lucky kid.

He sighed and dropped the phone to rub his face. Knuckling tired eyes was supposed to bad for the cornea, he remembered, but oh, it felt so good. He stood, pocketed the phone, and dropped his crumpled note in the trash. Now, to rehearsal. He headed down the corridor toward the auditorium, but his mind was elsewhere.

The caffeine gave his energy a little lift, but it didn't help the soul-crushing feeling of too much work and too little time. He'd never felt like this before. Busy was one thing, but now he felt like he was missing his life due to work. Heck, he'd always figured his work was his life. When he thought about this week, next week, all he could see was work and more work. No time to work with Mackenzie on their renovations, hike with her, watch old movies or read books together. No time to play with the dog, or visit with friends. He was stuck.

Stuck. He stretched his arms over his head as he walked, but still felt it. Like speeding down a big highway without any exits. All you can do is go as fast as possible and hope you get somewhere before the gas runs out.

It stank. It felt kind of familiar, but not good. This life just didn't fit him any more.

He still wanted to be a novelist, that was for sure. *And I want my life with Mackenzie. But how do I do that?*

The fatigue blossomed into sadness. He imagined each of them floating in a grey sea of separateness, reaching for each other, but always missing. In his mind, their home, the old farmhouse, sat empty, Mackenzie back in Boston and him some place he couldn't even imagine. His chest hurt with the sadness of that image.

We could be so happy. I've needed her for my entire life. She's here and I'm too busy working. If this relationship fails, it will absolutely be my fault. But there wasn't really time to think about that now, as he joined the horde of adolescents descending to the auditorium. He was needed here.

As soon as Mackenzie's car started down the long driveway to the dog sanctuary, she could hear barking. Murphy stood in the backseat, tail spinning. She parked beside a big blue van with a dog painted on the side, then dug around in the backseat for a leash.

Dorie came out of the old red barn. "Mackenzie! Hi!" She opened the back door of the car to release the dog. "Hey, Murph. Lots of new friends here." She grinned at Mackenzie, who still held the now useless leash. "He'll be fine," she said. "Come meet the gang."

Mackenzie followed Dorie to the play yard populated by a half dozen dogs large and small. Some peered through the fence, and it seemed all of them were barking. She squatted by the fence, Murphy beside her. "Look at you. You're pretty cute," she told a hairy-looking creature with bright black eyes peeking through a forelock. "You, too," she said to an animated mop. She poked her fingers through the fence, and Murphy touched noses with a larger dog.

"They're friendly," she commented, turning back to Dorie.

"This is the friendly play yard," Dorie said. "Some dogs don't do well with a crowd, so we have space for them elsewhere. Come on in." She led the way to the barn door.

Mackenzie gazed upward at the wooden sign. "Best Friends Dog Sanctuary," she read aloud. "That name says a lot."

"Yeah," Dorie agreed, giving Murphy's ears a good rubbing. "We want to make a good life for dogs whose owners can't keep them, and who aren't likely to be adopted."

"Why not?"

"Mostly because they're old or need a lot of medical care. We basically provide a service for people who need care for themselves. When we can, we take dogs to visit their people in care."

Dorie pushed open the door, and they entered. Mackenzie looked around the inside. A desk with a lamp, a coffeemaker, and a rug made a little office. It was a strange office, though, because the rug held a big black potato that turned out to be a sleeping pug, and there were divided spaces with cots that held sleeping dogs. The place was warm, clean, and slightly untidy. Mackenzie loved it.

"This is so much nicer than I ever imagined," she said, taking the offered chair. Dorie poured coffee for them both.

"I like it." She parked herself on the other chair, coffee for each of them on the desk. "We've been working on it for awhile now, and things are pretty good."

"This is your full-time work?"

"More than full time," she said with a laugh. "Chad works here, too, but for pay, he does freelance videography. He's really a filmmaker in disguise."

"It's so vibrant here."

"There's a lot of energy. Dogs are good like that. But you know about that because of Murphy."

Murphy, hearing his name, wandered over from nosing the pug potato and put his head on Dorie's knee. She bent down to smile at him, scritching his ears.

"This is my third coffee this afternoon," Mackenzie said. "It's a good thing caffeine doesn't keep me awake."

"Nothing keeps me awake," Dorie stated. "Coffee is a gift to the world, and we should make good use of it. That's a Madison family slogan."

"This is nice," Mackenzie said. "Just to see you here."

"My native environment. It's always a challenge, though, making sure we have funding to keep this place running. I've been thinking about your festival."

"It's not mine, but what are you thinking?"

"I'm always looking for ways to let people know about Best Friends. We need donations, volunteers, and we get our dogs by word-of-mouth as much as through social services. Would it be crazy to have a float?"

"Full of dogs?"

Dorie's face fell. "Yeah, that does sound crazy. Besides, some of these guys don't do well in crowds."

"What about driving your van in the parade? You could decorate it with lights and stuff, and hand out flyers."

"Yes!" Dorie fist-pumped. "That's a great idea. Thank you. We'll do that."

They smiled at each other. "I wanted to offer to help you, too," Dorie added. "We're not downtown and we're not a business, we're a non-profit, but I think we're an important part of the community. Is there something else you need done? I'm happy to help. Or volunteer my father."

"That's a great offer," Mackenzie said. "I've got a running list in the car. Maybe we can look at it together."

Thursday - 9 days until Sea Stars

Thursday was another long day sorting details in the village. Mackenzie was happy to have an invitation for her evening meal, even though she wondered if she'd finagled it by inviting Kathy for coffee. Kathy was too busy to take time off for coffee, but she had to feed voracious teens, so supper was a sure bet. She never seemed to mind setting an extra place.

Mackenzie dropped Murphy off at home, and then drove to her sister's farmhouse just down the road from hers.

"Dinner!" called Kathy up the stairs, after depositing a bowl of mashed potatoes on the harvest table. "Can you run up and get them?" she asked Mackenzie. "They've probably got headphones on."

"Sure," Mackenzie agreed, heading up the wooden stairs. She heard the kitchen door open and leaned down to say hello to Jake, her brother-in-law.

"Hey, Mack," he said. "How's that festival stuff coming?"

"Oh, it's coming," she said lightly. "I'll tell you all about it. I'm going to get the boys."

Upstairs, the narrow hallway of the old farmhouse was lit only by the faint dusk from the window at the end of the hall. She knew her way, anyway, and banged on one bedroom door and then another.

"What?" said Terence, bursting out his bedroom door. "Oh, hi, Mackenzie. I thought you were Mum."

"It's okay to be rude if I'm your mother?" She laughed. "Dinner's ready. Where's Tate?"

"Here I am," came a voice from down the hall. "Hiya, Mackenzie. What's it like living with an English teacher?"

"Come on down, you guys," she said, ignoring the question. Tate asked that every time they got together. "Dinner. Your dad's home."

She walked decorously back down the stairs but was followed by a tumble of teenage feet and arms and elbows and squabbling.

"Wash up," Jake said automatically.

"Hello to you, too, Dad," Terence said. "I washed up."

"You did not," Tate argued. "Liar."

Terence grabbed him and they wrestled to the floor, while Kathy walked around them to put a platter of ham and a basket of biscuits on the table.

"Come on, you two," she said. "You act like a couple of twelve-year-olds. Do you need to do a lap around the house before you sit down?"

One of the boys giggled and headed into the downstairs bathroom to wash up, while the other dangled his hands under the kitchen tap.

"It never ends," Kathy said. "I keep thinking they're almost grown up, but they prove me wrong at every opportunity. Can you get the green beans, please?"

"Of course," Mackenzie said and returned to the kitchen.

Terence had the beans in his hands and winked at her. "I've got this." She grinned back at him and followed him to the dining room where the family assembled around the table.

The food smelled wonderful. Mackenzie felt suddenly ravenous, but one more thing had to happen. Jake reached to each side, and the five of them held hands around the table. Jake closed his eyes.

"A moment of thanks, for good food, good family, and the opportunities we have to help each other." He opened his eyes. Mackenzie felt a squeeze in her left hand and tears welled up, as they always did. She passed the squeeze to the right. A moment later, Jake said, "Let's eat," and passed the platter of ham in her direction.

"You said leftovers, Kath. These are pretty elegant leftovers," Mackenzie commented.

"It is leftovers. We had a big ham on the weekend, and so this is leftover ham."

Mackenzie scoffed. "Plus potatoes, beans, biscuits..."

Kathy grinned at her. "Boys. I have boys to feed."

"What do you mean, Mum?" asked Tate, filling his plate. "You make it sound like a bad thing."

Terence elbowed him. "Only because of you. Not because of me." He grinned cheerfully at Mackenzie.

"Knock it off and eat your dinner," Jake admonished. "You both know your appetites are the stuff of legend."

"Right! That's us, the stuff of legend," Tate chortled.

Tucking into their food, the twins subsided enough for Kathy to say, "So, Mackie, tell us about the festival. How's it going?"

"Good, I think," she replied. "We're getting the parade lined up, and we've got a decent sized giveaway basket. Josiah Steeves is going to lead a food drive."

Jake raised his eyebrows. "Josiah is giving food away? Does Estelle know?"

Mackenzie smiled. "I was the only one who didn't know his reputation. He's launching the drive, and the collection will happen in his store."

Terence laughed. "People buy from him and then donate it? That's a deal for him."

"Maybe. But it does give people a chance to do something good," Kathy opined.

"People will do good things if we make it easy, according to Magda," Mackenzie said. "I didn't realize there was a food insecurity problem in Stella Mare."

"There is always a need," Jake said somberly.

"Estelle was not exactly enthusiastic."

Tate laughed out loud. "I bet. She's just mean. Yells at all the kids who go into the store."

Jake raised his eyebrows. "It's kids who shoplift for kicks, Tate, and if you had to deal with that, you might not be too nice either."

Tate frowned. "She treats everybody like they're a shoplifter. Hardly anybody does, though."

Kathy gave the twins a sidelong glance. "Estelle can be difficult, that's true," she said. "I think it helps to know a little about her."

"Everybody's got a story," Terence said. "That's what Mum always says. Walk a mile in their shoes and all that."

"What's Estelle's story?" Mackenzie wanted to know.

Kathy looked at Jake.

He looked back. "This is all you, Kath. I don't know much about it."

"Well, it was before my time," Kathy said. "But Dad told us about it."

Because Mackenzie hadn't grown up with Eric, she loved hearing his stories. "You've got my attention now," she said. "What happened?"

"Estelle was married very young, long before Josiah. She married a young French fella, I don't even know if I ever knew his name. Fisherman. Anyway, he was a youngster, and she was a youngster and they got married. Antoine, maybe."

"And?" Mackenzie wanted to hear this story.

"Well, this was back when Dad was young, and all the young guys would just pick up and go fishing with whoever would have them, just to make a few bucks. Anyway, it was a terrible thing; a winter storm came on suddenly. The boat capsized out in the middle of the Bay. Two men were never recovered, but the rest of them were okay."

"Another story about fishermen dying in the Bay of Fundy. I had no idea it was so dangerous," Mackenzie said.

Jake gave a short laugh. "You can die fishing anywhere, but yes, that's a big body of water. Storms, tides, all the usual things apply."

"Anyway," Kathy continued, "it was about this time of year. Estelle lost Antoine, so young."

"That's terrible," Mackenzie said. She thought about Estelle, tight-faced at her desk.

"That's not the whole of it, either," Jake added. "It was like bad luck followed that lady. She and Antoine had a child, born after his father died, but the baby died young, too. Before a year, I think."

Mackenzie's heart twisted. "Poor Estelle."

Kathy added, "People in the village were unkind, of course, saying things like it was for the best, otherwise he'd have no father, all that sort of claptrap."

"This must have been forever ago," Mackenzie said, trying to figure. "You weren't even born then. How do you know so much?"

"Oh, that's the village, too," Kathy said with a laugh. "You've been here long enough to know. People talk. Mostly about other people."

"Estelle lost her husband and her child. That's so sad."

"Yes. And some time later she married Josiah, who's not exactly sweetness and light."

"Maybe I can understand her edges." Mackenzie's chest tightened. Poor Estelle.

Kathy chuckled. "Understand, sure, but she's still a challenge. You know that love-your-neighbour stuff? It's not easy with her. But Josiah seems to love her, so she must have some redeeming qualities."

"She's critical of everything I bring to the Village Marketing meetings," Mackenzie said. "I'm from away, you know, and have foreign ideas."

Jake laughed. "That you do. There's nothing like new ideas to shake things up."

"New ideas are good," Terence said.

"You bet they are," Jake agreed. "That's why you young people are our hope for a good future. You have the new ideas."

Mackenzie frowned. "I'm not all that young, and my ideas aren't even new. Nothing we're doing is original or ground-breaking."

Tate giggled. "Maybe it is in Stella Mare, Mackie. If they never did it before then it's ground-breaking."

"Are you kids in high school doing ground-breaking stuff?" Mackenzie liked hearing her nephews talk about their lives.

"Well, kinda," he said. "Our float for the parade is about climate change. Some people in town still don't think it's even real."

"Yeah," added Terence. "Our adviser wanted us to just do a Christmas tree, but we said there won't be Christmas if we ruin our planet for humans."

"Well, it's hard to argue that point," Kathy agreed, stacking up plates. "Anybody want dessert?"

"Me! I'll help." Tate leaped up to take the plates to the kitchen. Mackenzie looked at the empty platters and bowls in awe.

"Those kids can eat," she said.

"That they can," Jake agreed, sliding his chair back. "They'll be starving by bedtime too."

"I was sixteen once, but I don't think I ever had that kind of appetite," she said, looking toward the kitchen.

"You were never a sixteen-year-old boy who was growing an inch a month and playing basketball every day," Kathy pointed out. "I remember this stage from their brother, but with two of them, the grocery bill is a shock. It's a good thing I bake."

Tate returned to the table with a pie. "This it, Mum?" he asked. "I saw cookies, too."

"Cookies are for later," she said. "Pie is tonight. Plates?"

"Oh, right," he said.

"I'll get them," Terence said helpfully. "Forks, too, right?"

"And the pie server," his mother reminded.

He returned, bearing dishes, cutlery, and a carton of ice cream. "Just in case anybody needed ice cream," he said with a grin. The boys served huge slices of pie, piled with creamy vanilla.

Mackenzie stared at her plate. "Thanks, guys," she said, "but I don't think..."

"Don't worry," Kathy assured her. "It will never go to waste in this house. The dishwashers will see to that."

Tate gave her a broad grin, matched by his twin.

"You two are something," Mackenzie said. "But what if I eat it all?"

Terence mimed tears and Mackenzie giggled. "To change the subject, do you guys want to help us out with little kid crafts at the Festival? Or can you volunteer a friend?"

"Sure. Maybe Tate's girlfriend will do it," Terence said with a wicked smile.

"Right. Maybe your girlfriends," Tate snapped back.

Before a fight could break out, Mackenzie asked, "Who are these girlfriends?"

"Yes, I'd like to know, too," Kathy said.

"Oh, nobody," Tate said.

"Tate likes Justine."

"I do not."

"Yes, you do. I know it."

Before the squabble could become anything more, Jake said firmly, "Finish your dessert and get the kitchen cleaned up. I need to see homework before you two go to bed. Got it?"

"Yes, sir," the twins said, stuffing in last bites, and then taking dishes to the kitchen.

The three adults sat for a moment in the relative quiet. "They're such good kids," Mackenzie said.

Kathy scoffed. "They're great kids. But a handful."

"I was worse," Jake noted. "I don't have any complaints."

Kathy gazed at him fondly. "You were a lot worse."

"Did you guys know each other at that age?"

Kathy laughed. "Of course we did. You know how big Declan's school is, right? It was even smaller when we went there."

"Did you date in high school?"

Jake laughed. "She was the prettiest girl in school. She wasn't going to have much to do with a mess like me."

"You were a mess, that's for sure," Kathy agreed. She turned to Mackenzie. "Jake was one of those kids smoking weed under the bleachers. The kind your mother told you to stay away from."

"No kidding." She looked at Jake. "I can't see it, Jake. You just have that clean cut thing going on now."

"I know. But in my heart, I'm really into leather and black hair dye and pasty skin that never saw the light of day. Weird piercings. Don't tell the boys."

"Really? In Stella Mare?"

He laughed. "It was a look. Hard to get that basement pallor when you had to work in the woods with your dad whenever you were out of school, but I worked it. Chains, black leather, and tattoos. You know, everyone has them now, but back then, well, it made me cool."

"He was so cool my mother wouldn't let me talk to him," Kathy added. "She was wary."

"What about Eric?" Mackenzie often wondered what kind of father Eric had been.

"Eric was why Mum was so cautious. She'd had a rough time with him when I was little. Things got better for her when he was out of the picture, but of course he kept reappearing."

Jake laughed again. "Eric thought I was just fine. Kathy's mum and Dean, her step-dad, disagreed."

"Eric bought weed from you," Kathy said grimly.

"That was only the once," Jake reminded. "Mackenzie, don't take this too seriously. Kathy's mum decided I was okay, we got married, and the rest is history."

"He makes it sound so easy," Kathy said, scoffing. "My mother didn't thaw toward him until after we were married. He'd gotten his pharmacy degree, lost the mohawk and leather, and had a good job, and she was still unconvinced."

"Simon was the clincher. When she held her first grandson, she decided I could stay," Jake said with some satisfaction. "I'm sorry you won't get to meet her, Mackie. She was a strong, proud lady."

Mackie felt her eyes smart. No, she wouldn't get to meet Kathy's mother and Kathy would never meet hers. In fact, neither mother would ever know there had been two daughters in Eric Johnson's life.

"That's a good story," she said to Jake. "I guess it takes some people a long time to accept change."

"Or to believe in lasting change," he said. "Kathy's mum assumed I was a screw-up adult because I'd been kind of a screwed-up kid."

"She came around," Kathy said. "That's the part to remember."

"Yeah." Mackenzie sighed. "Maybe Estelle will come around."

Kathy laughed and got up from the table. "I wouldn't hold my breath." She headed for the kitchen.

Jake looked at Mackenzie. "It's good that you're here. Good for everyone."

She smiled. "Thanks, Jake. I'm glad to be here."

Declan opened the kitchen door as quietly as possible, but Murphy leaped to welcome him, and Mackenzie called sleepily from the sitting room. Leaving his boots in the mudroom, he padded toward her blanket-swathed body. She moved over to make room for him on the couch in front of the pellet stove.

"Hi," he said, sliding in next to her.

"Mmmm," she murmured and leaned against him. "You're late."

"I sure am." He stifled a yawn. "Almost time to get up and do it all over again."

She sighed and snuggled in as he pulled her closer. "You're sleepy," he said.

"Yes, I am," she agreed. "Want to go to bed?"

"That sounds wonderful," he whispered into her hair. She leaned in, tucking her head under his chin with a little moan.

He sighed. "I have work to do."

She sat up abruptly. "What? Now?" The blanket fell off her as she pulled away from him.

He sighed. "Yeah, I know. But I won't sleep if I don't have these essays ready for tomorrow. You go ahead up."

She sighed. "I waited up for you."

With a stab of regret, he said, "I know you did. I'm really sorry."

"Sorry again," she said, standing up. "I don't think sorry is working for me, Declan." She shook her head and headed for the stairs.

"Mackenzie," he said, but quietly. "Please. Don't be mad. Things will improve."

She turned, hand on the newel post. "You've been saying that all along. It's all good stuff, but it keeps you busy. It's who you are."

"No, wait, it's the situation. Things will get better."

"When, Declan? After the holidays, you're going to be writing again. You'll be at work all day, and at your desk all night."

He was silent. She wasn't wrong.

"I know you told me to expect this," she said.

"I've been told I'm not partner material, but I want that to change." He gazed at the floor. "I want our life — us — to work. I love you."

"I love you, too," she said. There was a long pause. Then, with an effort, she said, "I know how to be alone. I've done that most of my life."

"I don't want you to be alone," he said with alarm. What was she thinking?

She shrugged. "We're both good at doing our own things. I don't want to ask more than you want to give."

"I know I leave you alone a lot," he said. "I get caught up in writing, or work, or something."

She nodded. "We used to feel more connected, even though we were busy," she said. "I didn't think that was going to change when we moved in together. I thought living with you would be different."

"It is different," he said. "I'm different."

"Different how?"

"I'm different than I was," he said. "Like all this." He waved his arm. "I love all this. Our house, our being together. I never paid any attention before. Always just stuck on my writing, my work."

She paused, then gave a stiff nod. "Okay."

"What did you mean about being alone?" His voice cracked a bit.

She gazed away from him, her eyes filling. It was too quiet in the room.

"I know you still have the house in Boston," he said, "but stay. Please stay."

She turned a sharp glance on him. "I'm not going anywhere," she said firmly. "My family is here. I thought you were part of that."

He breathed out relief. "I am. We'll find a way to make it work."

"We won't find it this way," she said. "Each one going our own way, never crossing paths. Except for late-night conversations when we're too tired to think."

"We'll figure it out," he said, heart sinking. "We love each other, we want the same things."

"Could we just try to see each other more? I don't need a lot, but more than what we're doing now."

"In a week we can. Just another week," he promised, and saw her shoulders sag. He hurried on. "The play and festival will both be over. We'll have time to just be us, you and me."

"Okay. Sure," she said, sounding tired. "Goodnight." She slowly headed up the stairs, head down.

He watched her walk up the stairs, his chest and throat tight. *Don't leave me. Don't go. I can't bear it if you leave.* Standing, he rubbed his eyes, then his jaw. *I will make this work. I will.*

But change had to happen later. Right now, she needed sleep, and he had to work. Turning away, he headed for his little office, clicking on lamps as he went. Papers had to be marked. In his mind, he tucked Mackenzie safely into bed as he tried to settle into grading essays. Murphy lay across his feet like a rug.

Even though she'd been nearly asleep on the couch, when Mackenzie got upstairs, she was wide awake. The bed felt too big. Even Murphy had abandoned her to keep Declan company.

Her mind floated to long nights alone in a big bed when she'd been married before. Her ex-husband had been a "go-getter" according to Mackenzie's mother, who had approved wholeheartedly. Andrew had been committed to getting ahead, therefore he was rarely at home. Instead, he was working or schmoozing or golfing, and she was required for the occasional command performance as The Wife, when he made her dress up to be paraded around. Her chest tightened as she recalled one company party. It was such a relief to know that old life was gone. She had her own life now. Her life with Declan.

Declan would never treat her like a possession. He wasn't Andrew. But alone was alone. Alone reminded her of being a kid, watching reruns and eating her sandwich supper before opening multiple deadbolts to her mother, tired and irritable after working two jobs. So much time spent alone made her self-reliant, but her mother had preferred grateful and dependent. It was okay she made her own sandwich, but she didn't get to decide anything important about her life.

She sighed gustily, wanting to escape the painful memories. Even though Declan was downstairs working, she felt small and lonely in the big bed. What would Christmas be like? She'd have to pry him away from his laptop to have dinner. He'd sneak back into his office to work. She'd be exhausted and resentful, doing all the preparation. She could see it, clear as anything, and her ire rose.

Getting hot as she got angrier, she tossed aside the covers and got up to pace the room.

After two turns around on the wide pine boards, her skin was chilled, and she came to her senses. This is stupid, she thought finally. He's not a terrible human being and I don't have to tell myself stories about the future. He's just got to remember we're together now.

I need to remember that, too, she thought, feeling shame as she recalled her words at the foot of the stairs. Andrew had used threats, and her mother had used guilt. Even though it worked to keep her in line for a while, she didn't want to be that way with Declan. She'd practically been channelling her mother.

"Get thee behind me, Sarah," she muttered, and shook off the thought. No guilting, no threats. She climbed back into bed and snuggled deep under the duvet. It felt better there now. The floor was too cold for barefoot pacing, anyway.

Things with Dec would sort themselves out. They loved each other. They wanted the same things. He said so. She could decide to believe him.

She woke enough when he slipped in beside her to roll toward him. He wrapped his arms around her, murmuring in her ear. "I'm sorry, baby."

She snuggled into the curve of his shoulder, wrapping her arm over his hip. Before she could move again, he was snoring.

Friday - 8 days until Sea Stars

She got a text from school at midday.

Declan: *Let's invite Chad and Dorie for Saturday night. Sorry about, well, everything.*

Mackenzie: *I'll ask them. Dinner?*

Declan: *I can do lasagne.*

Mackenzie: *That's a nice offer, but I'll cook. You have rehearsal all morning. I'll invite them.*

He was trying, she thought. We're both trying. Her stomach felt settled for the first time all day. She sent a quick note of invitation to Dorie and got an instant and enthusiastic response, then returned to her festival organizing. The checklist never got shorter. As she ticked items off, more appeared.

Find Santa. That meant asking at the Sunshine Diner who knew Billy Seymour. The Sunshine patrons knew everything.

Confirm Santa suit with the costume company in St. Stephen.

Get groceries for weekend dinner guests.

Still thinking, she got ready for town, dressing for the cold. She had flyers, grocery bags, and the dog. She was all set.

After getting the lowdown from patrons at the Sunshine, Mackenzie drove down Fish House Road. She picked her way over rocks treacherous with ice to get to the fish houses. Mackenzie knew the area well, but instead of looking for her father, she was in search of another character of village renown, one Billy Seymour, her could-be Santa Claus. Russ Johnson, a long-time customer at the Sunshine, told her Billy would no doubt be located down fish house row. She felt the comfort of familiarity as she got out of the car and looked up with a practiced eye. This time of year, chimney activity signaled habitation. It was a couple of hours past high tide, so the fishing boats were all out. Only one shack bore a telltale stream of smoke. Billy Seymour – she hoped - was in. She rapped smartly on the door and stepped in.

"Hello?"

"Hey there," the man said. "You've come to the right place."

She laughed. "How do you know what I'm looking for?"

"Don't matter. You're here, and so you've come to the right place."

She closed the door behind her. "Nice and warm in here," she said. He was shoving a piece of wood into the pot-bellied stove. His white hair and beard suggested she had, indeed, come to the right place.

"Have ye a seat, me darlin'," he said, sitting himself and gesturing to a chair.

"I'm looking for Mr. Seymour," she said.

"You found him," he said. "Only I'm Billy."

"I'm Mackenzie," she said, keeping her hands in her lap.

"Eric Johnson's girl from the States, right?"

Surprised, she nodded. "How'd you know?"

"Oh, everybody knows something around here," he said. "What they know ain't always right, but they know it."

"Well, in this case, you're right. Yes, I'm Eric's daughter, the one from the States."

"And what can I do ye for, Eric's daughter?"

She wasn't sure how to broach the subject. "Do you have grandchildren, Billy?" she asked.

"That I do," he said. "Why do you want to know?"

"I bet they love your beard," she said.

He chuckled. "You're looking for a Santa, aren't ye?"

She laughed nervously. "You guessed it. How did you know?"

He scoffed. "Pretty young thing asking me about a white beard in December. Not too hard to figure out."

"Well, you got me," she said. "Yes, Billy, I'm asking if you'd be Santa for the Sea Stars Festival Parade. It's coming right up; it's next week on Saturday."

"Well, now, what's involved? It's been awhile since I been Santa."

"A costume, of course. You'd sit in a wagon and get carted around by draft horses since we don't have reindeer, and at the end of the parade, you would welcome everybody to the opening of the festival."

He scowled. "Like make a speech? I'm not too big on speeches."

"What about if I write it? And it's short, like Merry Christmas everyone and welcome. Ho ho ho! Let the festival begin!" She used her best big Santa-style voice.

The old man chuckled. "You could be Santa, you know."

"Nope. No beard."

"Okay. Is that all? I don't have to sit children on my lap or anything?"

"What would you think about children on your lap? We could do that, too, if you want."

His scowl returned. "Kids are fine, but not on my lap. I can do the parade bit, but not the lap bit."

"Okay," Mackenzie agreed. "We really just need you for the parade. That's wonderful, Billy, that you can do this. Now you'll have to be at the campground where the parade starts at three-thirty. Okay? I'll have the costume and the horses and wagon meet you there."

"You bet. I'm happy to do it." He pulled out a flask. "Care for a drink to seal the deal?"

She shook her head. "I'd take coffee, though."

"Well, I can make you a cup of tea." He got up to put the kettle on the wood stove.

"That sounds good," she said. "I think"—she rummaged in her big tote bag—"maybe I have a couple of doughnuts in here." The Sunshine had yielded more than just information. Doughnuts always sweetened a deal.

"Might hit the spot."

Her last stop of the day was the Save Mart, where she collected eggplant, ground lamb, cheese, tomatoes and staples for the house. The store was the quietest she'd ever seen it, and only one cash register was open. Her heart caught in her throat at the sight of Estelle at the register. She pushed her little cart into the lane and straightened her shoulders.

Piling her groceries on the conveyor, she waited while a lady with pink and white hair sorted through her change and chatted to Estelle. The lady turned to Mackenzie with a sweet smile.

"Sorry for taking so long, dear," she said. "Just trying to use up some of this change. Hardly anybody takes cash anymore, do they?"

Mackenzie smiled back. "It's fine," she said, and it was. She was in no hurry to talk to Estelle.

The lady left and Mackenzie took her place, while Estelle efficiently pulled the items across the scanner, her gaze never leaving the food. She said, a little absently, "Looks like moussaka."

"That's right," Mackenzie said, surprised.

At the sound of her voice, Estelle looked up, unsmiling. "Oh, it's you."

Mackenzie nodded. "Hi, Estelle," she said. "Do you make moussaka?"

Her face softened. "I used to. Mr. Vassilios had a little restaurant here in the sixties. I served tables and cleaned. Mrs. Vassilios taught me how to cook. They let me live out back for a while."

Mackenzie remembered Kathy's story about Estelle. Perhaps the Vassilios family took her in. "There's no Greek restaurant here now, is there?"

Estella had a faraway look. "No, not anymore. The Vassilioses left in the mid-seventies."

"Real Greek moussaka," Mackenzie mused. "I bet that's good."

"Do you use potatoes as well as eggplant?"

"Potatoes? No, but that sounds good."

Estelle gave her a quick look then said, "Wait right here," and bustled off into the store. Returning with some green sprigs and a round of white cheese in her hand, she slid them into Mackenzie's cloth shopping bag. "Here."

"What's that?"

Estelle leaned forward. "Fresh oregano and kefalotyri. The cheese. It will make a big difference. And use potatoes along with your eggplant."

"Thank you so much," Mackenzie said.

Estelle brushed her off. "If you're going to go to the trouble of making it, do it right, I always say."

"I'll let you know how it turns out," Mackenzie promised.

"Harrumph," Estelle said, quickly scanning the rest of the groceries. "Ninety-seven thirty-two," she announced.

Mackenzie paid and grabbed her bags. "Thank you again, Estelle," she said as she walked out. What a peculiar interaction. But a good one. She poked her nose into the bag to sniff at the oregano. This was going to be interesting.

Part III

Saturday - 7 days until Sea Stars

Saturday morning she called Magda. "Good morning. Sea Stars Central, checking in."

"Hey. You're in a good mood."

"Fake it 'til you make it. I just panicked, realizing I never got Kevin's number from you. I haven't called him yet. And the parade's getting bigger."

"Bigger?"

"We now have fourteen groups coming, including five floats, a dance team, a band, and the pipes and drums, and of course Santa."

"Yes, so we really need Kevin Ellison. He ran the Sea Cadets. I'll ask him if you like."

"That would be very helpful. Give him my number, please." Mackenzie's chest loosened slightly. "It's pretty short notice."

"I'm sure he'll help. He loves these community events."

"Should we have invited the Sea Cadets? I don't even know what Sea Cadets are."

"No worries. This is our first year. We're entitled to all our lapses."

"Really? I don't want to make anybody mad."

"Don't worry so much! Nobody will be mad. You're doing fine."

"I saw Estelle yesterday," Mackenzie blurted out. "She was almost nice."

"No way," scoffed Magda. "Not Estelle."

"Really. She gave me some recipe tips."

"Hmm. Maybe she likes you," Magda said, though she sounded doubtful.

"It made me take another look at that flyer she gave me," Mackenzie said. "I still don't really understand, but it's something about women widowed in fishing accidents, back in the 1960s."

"Really? She must have been pretty young back then."

"I think we should talk about it," Mackenzie said. "Maybe next week."

Candlelight illuminated the tabletop and allowed the old plaster walls to fade into the shadows. Mackenzie surveyed the vase of red dogwood stems and white pine branches Declan had gathered from their woods, the mismatched table settings of antique and handcrafted plates, and the steaming food. Declan, pouring wine into their guest's glasses, looked up at her with a smile. This was just right. Friends, good food, and good conversation.

"Estelle was nice?" Dorie, flabbergasted, chewed appreciatively. "Oh, this is really good," she added. "Chad, we need this recipe."

Chad shook his head. "Dorie, getting a recipe won't make us into cooks."

"It's pretty good," Mackenzie agreed, tasting critically. "Warming food for chilly nights."

"Speaking of which," Declan said, "will you look at the pellet stove with me later, Chad? I don't know if things are working right."

"Ha," said Dorie. "A guy thing, no doubt."

Chad grinned. "Sure, Dec, whatever. I have no idea about pellet stoves, but I'll help you look. We can be all manly and stuff."

"I suppose the girls get to do the dishes," Dorie said scathingly.

"Maybe we'll just retire to the parlour for cigars and brandy," Declan said. "Leave you little ladies to your own devices."

"Did I tell you somebody called me 'little lady' to my face the other day?" Mackenzie asked.

"I'm not surprised," Dorie said. "This is Stella Mare, after all. My father might do something like that."

Chad shook his head. "Give him more credit. I think four daughters have taught James a thing or two. He might have gotten away with that a decade ago, but not now."

"Where'd that happen?" Declan asked curiously. "Down at the docks?"

"No, but that's a good guess. It was Josiah at the Save Mart. He pointedly asked if we were married, too," Mackenzie added. She didn't add he'd nearly called her a bastard.

The other three hooted with laughter. "Did he shame you?" Dorie asked. "Like you need a scarlet letter or something?"

When they finished laughing, Mackenzie mused, "It must be a little hard to hold things dear and have the rest of the world move on."

"I think marriage is important. Not necessary, but important," Dorie said. "Me and Chad, you know, we're planning to get married. It means something to me."

"It's no longer a prerequisite to sharing a house," Declan said. "Thank goodness."

Chad and Dorie laughed again, but Mackenzie was quiet. "Come on, Dec," Dorie teased. "You're not opposed to marriage, are you?"

"Opposed? No. I'm happy you two are getting married."

"When is that, anyway?" Mackenzie asked. "Do you have a date?"

Dorie raised eyebrows in Chad's direction. "We have no idea," he said. "Sometime. We're too busy right now to even think about it, really. But we will."

"What about you, Mackenzie?" Dorie asked. "Are you opposed to marriage as an institution?"

"Not at all," she said. "I might have a different perspective, though. I've been married."

"Oh, you have," Dorie said breathlessly. "Been there, done that?"

"It was long ago; feels like a lifetime ago," she admitted. Except when the loneliness hits, she thought, but did not say.

Thankfully, Dorie changed the subject and regaled them with a funny story about a new dog at the sanctuary, but Mackenzie was only half paying attention. She and Declan had never spoken about marriage. She wondered where he really stood.

After dessert, Declan and Mackenzie walked out to the driveway with Chad and Dorie. Murph headed for the woods, and Mackenzie wrapped her arms around her shoulders against the chill. "This is one of those Maritime things that I like," she said to Dorie. "Nobody says goodbye at the door. Always from here."

"The dooryard, you mean," Chad said. "This is the dooryard."

"Right," Mackenzie said with a smile. "That was a new term, too."

"Well, we're saying goodbye from the dooryard tonight," Declan said. "Thanks guys, for coming over."

"It was great," Dorie said. "Next time, you come to us, though."

"Sorry about that, Dorie. I just couldn't get out in time yesterday," Declan said.

"No problem," she said airily. "Moussaka makes up for anything." She climbed into the truck.

"Good night," Chad called from his open window, and the truck trundled down the driveway as they waved.

Mackenzie turned toward the woods to call Murphy and gasped. "Dec, look at the moon!"

The big orb hung just above the midnight-black spruces. There was a glow like a halo around it. An owl hooted somewhere in the forest.

"Hm, beautiful," Declan said, reaching for Mackenzie with one arm. "It's full tomorrow. A super moon."

"I don't even know what that means," Mackenzie said. "It's lovely."

"It sure is," Declan said. She turned to look at him and instead of looking at the moon, he was gazing at her face. "This was such a nice evening," he said. "Thank you for making it happen."

Declan was the perfect boyfriend when it suited him, she thought perversely, her warm feelings marred by a stab of irritation. Stay in the moment, she thought, and smiled at him. "You're welcome. I hope we can have more friends over."

"I do too," he said. "I enjoy being a couple."

She studied his face. "Do you? Are you sure?" A shiver overtook her.

"Let's get you inside," he said. "It's getting colder out here."

He shepherded her toward the kitchen door while calling to the dog. "Murph!"

"He'll be along," she said.

"You go in," he urged. "You're getting chilled. I'll wait for him."

She pushed open the door to a spill of welcome light and warmth. The kitchen was tidy, dishwasher running quietly and music coming from the sitting room. She wandered to the sink to fill the kettle, then set it back on the hob, empty. Tired. She was tired.

Where was Dec? She leaned out the door and saw him walking toward the woods, Murphy at his side. Maybe he had some thinking to do. Maybe she did, too. She headed up to bed, remembering he hadn't answered her question. Was he sure he wanted to be a couple? Was she, for that matter?

Sunday - 6 days until Sea Stars

Declan was busy with grading, so on Sunday afternoon Mackenzie took Murphy out for a hike. It was freezing cold, and the wind spit flurries into her face as she crossed the cut-over hayfield. She reached the wooded trail with relief and settled into a steady pace under the wind-blocking canopy. The dog ranged around sniffing.

Walking helped her think. The trail narrowed, and she picked her way over the rocks that jutted through the thin soil. The sound of water running over rocks tugged at her attention, and she leaned over a small ravine to check on the brook. When would it ice over?

She clambered down the bank to squat beside the little stream, poking at the ice along its edges with a stick. Murphy scrambled down beside her, then delicately tiptoed across the water.

"Cold paws, buddy," she warned, but it didn't matter, not really. Absently, she dropped a desiccated leaf on the water and watched it bump up against the frozen edge, then slip away with the current as the water pushed it just a little harder. Soon the cold would overtake the stream, freezing it solid. Leaves caught then would be stuck in the same place until spring. For some reason she thought of Josiah, rigid neck and jutting chin, and just as suddenly, an image of her mother Sarah overlaid him. Rising abruptly, she called to the dog and climbed back up the hill to continue her hike.

Walking, she shook out her shoulders and arms, then broke into a run. Murphy, excited by her change in mood, leaped up. "Come on, Murph! Let's have fun!" She ran until she felt tired, then ran a little more. Finally exhausted, she headed back toward the farmhouse, Murphy in her wake.

After her shower, she sat at the laptop looking at her list for the festival. Like magic, Magda called, slightly breathless. "Mackenzie? Volunteer firefighters in the parade."

"Oh, my goodness. How could I forget them?" Declan was part of the local brigade.

"I'm sending you the chief's number. Those guys love to be out in the public, especially where there are kids."

"Kids love firetrucks, too," she added. "Thanks. Thanks so much."

"Dec," she called toward his office. "I forgot the fire brigade."

"What?" He came to the doorway.

"I can't believe it. I forgot to invite them."

"Sorry. I should have thought of it," he said regretfully.

"Not your fault," she said. "But embarrassing, for sure."

"It'll be okay," he said. "Probably."

She called Chief Legrand immediately. He was delighted to hear from her despite the short notice. "We can hand out fire safety flyers," he said cheerily. "Do you know how many fires get started on the holidays? People leave candles burning all over."

"Really?" Mackenzie said, sidling to the kitchen counter to blow out a pine-scented pillar candle.

"Oh, yes," he said learnedly, "it is a big problem. We love to talk about prevention."

"Well, thank you. Do you think you'll have a truck for the parade?"

"Well, yes, as a matter of fact. We're doing the Santa parade in St. Stephen in the morning, but we're available Saturday afternoon. You want us to carry Santa?"

Mackenzie's imagination flared. "Santa on the fire truck?"

"We do that some places," he commented.

"Well, this year we've got a wagon and horses for him," she said, "but I'll keep that in mind for the future."

"You do that. You're Declan's girl, ain't you?"

"Yes, that's right."

"When I heard about this here parade, I was some surprised you didn't start with the firefighters, but he told me you're from away."

"Well, yes, I am, but..."

"That's okay, then, and now we understand each other. The volunteer firefighters will always do whatever we can for Stella Mare."

"Thank you, Chief," she said. "Now I know."

She hung up and paced the kitchen, giggling. As long as I'm from away, he can understand my faux pas, she thought. Maybe it's a good thing I have this excuse for bad behaviour at the ready.

Monday - 5 days until Sea Stars

The Monday morning before the festival, Declan took his coffee to the kitchen table. Mackenzie was there, owl-eyed, staring into her mug. She looked up at he sat.

"Breakfast at home today?" she asked.

"I have a couple of minutes. I wanted to talk about this week." It was better to let her know upfront. No crushed expectations.

"Go ahead." She leaned back in her chair.

"This is the big week. Open dress rehearsal for families on Wednesday. You're welcome to come, of course," he added. "You're welcome at any rehearsal."

"Okay," she said mildly.

"Then opening night Thursday, big audience expected for Friday, closing night Saturday. Probably everyone in town who hasn't seen the show by Saturday will be there."

"The entire village comes out for the high school play?"

"Usually," he said. "The kids have their cast party right after the Saturday show."

"It's also the Sea Star Ball, Dec. There's the parade, the downtown stuff, the play, then the Ball. The Ball is even at the high school. Isn't that also the cast party?"

"The official one, yes," he said. "The kids will probably party on their own, too."

"I wondered about that. I didn't think kids would like to go to a dance with adults."

"If the official party is the Sea Stars Ball, that's good," Declan said. "Do you have a date?"

She giggled through her fatigue. "Honestly, I can't even think that far ahead. All I know is I'm not responsible for the Ball."

"So will you be my date for the Ball?" He waggled his eyebrows. "The play will be over, the festival will be done, and we can just have some fun."

"I'm not sure I have anything to wear," she demurred. He gave her a sideways glance. "Okay, that's an excuse. Sure, I'd be happy to be your date at the Ball."

"Great. Now we just have to get through this last week of preparation."

"We'll be worn out from trying to get everything done all at once."

"You sound exhausted already," he said sympathetically. "We need some holiday spirit. Next weekend is full of fun things for everyone."

She smiled weakly. "I'm waiting for the spirit to hit me. I hope it doesn't wait until after Christmas. I just feel so responsible."

"You know, it doesn't have to be perfect. It's a hometown event with hometown folks."

"I don't want to let anyone down."

"Let me help on Saturday. I'll have to be at school by five or so, but I can help before then. Assuming no last-minute play disasters."

"Thank you. That means a lot. I'm sure the festival will have some disaster or six."

"Keep me in mind," he said confidently. "I've got to go now, though. It's going to be okay. Really."

"That's what I keep telling myself," she said. "Not just about the festival. About us."

His stomach clenched. "Mackenzie?"

She looked up but didn't smile. "I'm not trying to be difficult. I'm just feeling my way in this relationship. We're new to living together, still."

He looked down. "I know. I'm going to do better."

"It's not about you doing anything better. I see you trying, but you're working as hard as you can. Maybe we're just not a good fit, you and me." Her voice caught on the words.

His throat clenched. "Mackenzie, don't say that. Please." He got up and grabbed his coat. "Things are going to be good, really."

He filled his travel mug from the carafe. "I have to go." His eyes smarted. "Don't give up on us. Please."

He opened the door to a gust of freezing wind.

Declan's pained expression wasn't lost on Mackenzie. He was right, they both wanted the same things. Love, connection, and a sense of family. For the first time, she wondered if Declan had the same feelings about family she did. She'd assumed his many cousins and his loving aunt and uncle filled up any empty places, but he had lost his father and then his mother when he was a little boy. Both of them were good at being alone, and neither of them had any experience in being together, being a couple. No wonder they were struggling.

She recognized his efforts, having Chad and Dorie over, offering to help on Saturday. Maybe she could try harder. Meet him halfway. At least halfway. She'd go to rehearsal this afternoon.

She turned to her work with a lighter spirit. It was the homestretch. Everything had to come together on Saturday. She opened her laptop.

Festival details felt tidied up until yet another crisis arose. Most she could manage by phone or online, but constantly putting out fires was exhausting.

By two p.m., Mackenzie needed to get out of the house. Maybe it was the extra coffee, or perhaps just nervous energy, but she needed to move. Leaving Murphy asleep on his dog bed, she drove into the village, parking at the Save Mart. Time to give the devil his due. Or her due, as the case may be.

Entering the store, she looked at the check-out lines. Estelle was there, talking to one of the cashiers. Mackenzie tucked her hands into her sleeves and approached.

"Estelle?"

The older woman gave her a sharp glance, then said, "Just a minute." Mackenzie busied herself looking at the cigarettes behind the plastic barrier, trying hard not to eavesdrop. In a moment, Estelle gestured for her to follow and led the way into the office.

"So?"

"I just wanted to tell you about the moussaka. It was the best I ever made, and maybe the best I ever had. I think it was the cheese," Mackenzie said. "Thank you."

Estelle lifted her chin. "The potatoes, too," she said. "That's part of the secret."

"Well, I'll never go back," Mackenzie told her. "It was so good. I just wanted to tell you. Thank you."

Estelle nodded. "I heard you that day, you know."

"What do you mean?"

"I heard you telling Josiah about your mum, back in Boston."

"Oh." Mackenzie flushed. What had she said?

"I thought you were some stuck-up rich city girl before that," Estelle said. "How you doing with the widows and orphans?"

Mackenzie thought furiously. "I couldn't read much of that paper, to be honest. It was faded."

"Yeah, we all are," Estelle murmured, causing Mackenzie to lean closer. "See if you can help. You understand the need."

"Okay," Mackenzie said, uncomprehending. "I'll look into it."

"Josiah thinks people should just forget. I would have died if not for the Vassiliakos," Estelle said, suddenly fervent. "People need help."

"Yes," Mackenzie agreed. She knew they could agree on that, but the rest of this conversation was beyond her. "Thank you."

Estelle nodded and turned toward her desk.

"Goodbye," Mackenzie said, but Estelle didn't even look up.

Still bemused, Mackenzie drove down Water Street past Market Square and up the hill toward the high school. It was hard to imagine in only five days the village would be transformed for the Sea Stars Festival. Now in late fall, light was gloomy as the daylight waned, shadows long even when the sun remained bright just above the horizon. A single bus departed the parking lot as she pulled in.

The auditorium was dark except for the stage, where kids milling about made a steady hum of activity. She slipped into a seat in the back, sliding down in the chair.

Monday's rehearsal was an exercise in barely controlled chaos. Hammering behind the stage made speeches hard to hear, kids scattered throughout the auditorium chatting, and Pat watched from the front, sometimes leaping to her feet. Mackenzie, settled into her back row seat, watched the kids stumble over lines and props disappear and reappear with dizzying speed (generally in the wrong place). Two girls emerged from backstage with a bundle of tulle. Going to consult with Declan, they spread it across a row of auditorium seats. If that was a costume, it had a long way to go before Thursday. Pat called up to where the lights were being operated, giving more directions. Before turning back, she squinted into the dark toward the back row. Mackenzie waved and she returned it, then walked toward Declan, speaking into his ear.

He glanced back and Mackenzie waved again. He grinned, and gestured for her to come to the front, but before she could move, a click click click of heels sounded to her right and a blonde woman in a suit tugged on Declan's sleeve. He turned to follow her up the aisle as Pat called, "Okay, everybody, let's take it from the beginning of this scene." The chaos on stage intensified then died down.

The blonde woman and Declan faced each other halfway up the aisle. Mackenzie watched, fascinated.

Long blonde hair barely moved as the woman leaned close to Dec's face. Talking, she touched his shoulder, then his arm. He backed up slightly, looking toward her in the darkness of the auditorium. She waved again, his face lit up and he walked her way.

"Hi!" he whispered, as the play was ongoing, but his delight was apparent. "You came. That's great!" He gestured to her to come out to the aisle.

Drawn in by his smile, she slid toward him, and was wrapped in a big hug. He whispered into her ear, "Save me from my vice principal." Then he turned toward the woman in heels. "This is my girlfriend Mackenzie," he said, holding onto her. "This is Aurora Smithers, vice principal. She's a big supporter of the drama club."

Ms. Smithers gave her a brief nod.

"Hi, Aurora," Mackenzie said. She tamped down her desire to give her a sharp kick. It might feel good, but the woman was Declan's boss. Sort of. "Nice to meet you."

"You, too. Declan, you'll keep me posted, of course."

"Of course," he agreed. She tapped up the aisle and out.

Dec spun around to look at Mackenzie, grinning. "Come on down and sit with Pat and me," he said. "See things from the director's point of view."

She demurred, but he persisted. "Come on. It's the best view."

When they returned to his row, Pat MacRae leaned over to give Mackenzie a hug. "It's so nice to see you," she said. "I know Dec's been here instead of at home."

Mackenzie shrugged. "It's work. I get it."

The three settled in to watch Chuck muff his lines for the third time, the King to slip and fall on a slippery bit of floor, and lighting changes to happen at random. Declan had a firm hold of her hand and kept looking at her with pleasure and delight. Maybe things were at least okay between them. Maybe even good. It was a shame she'd waited so long to see a rehearsal.

However, she was technically still at work, so when her phone vibrated in her pocket, she trotted out to the lobby to take the call. Kevin Ellison was calling about the parade. She hoped for good news.

"Hi, Kevin. Maybe I should start by apologizing," she said.

A laugh rumbled in his voice. "For what?"

"I just heard you run the Sea Cadets, and I didn't invite them to the parade. But I never heard of Sea Cadets before."

He chuckled. "No worries. I don't do that anymore, and besides, there was a notice in the local paper. I could have called you. Now what is it you need from me?"

"Magda said you'd be good on the front end, organizing," she said, feeling optimistic.

"Well, maybe," he said. "What do you have so far?"

She opened her notebook. "We have fourteen groups. No, fifteen, with the firefighters. Two musical groups including the bagpipers, two dance groups, and five floats, plus the firetruck, and Santa's wagon. We start at the campground, parade through town on Water Street, then stop at Market Square for Santa to wish everyone Merry Christmas. The parade will head to the high school to disband, but also so everyone can go to the play."

She could hear a scribbling pencil. "I assume that Santa goes last?"

"That's what I thought, yes," she said.

"Okay. That's great. Can you send me the files? I'll plan the lineup, organize with the campground, and do the communications to the folks in the parade. They'll need to get at the set-up an hour early, and we'll have to get them out of the school parking lot at least half an hour before the play starts, so there's room for audience parking."

Mackenzie felt her shoulders dropping as she heard this kind, authoritative voice taking over. "You know exactly what to do," she said. "You have no idea how much of a relief this is."

He chuckled again. "It's not hard. Just a lot of details and communication."

"Thank you so much, Kevin," she said. "You are taking such a load off my shoulders."

"I actually like this stuff. It's going to be chaos," he warned, "but it'll be an organized chaos. Just be prepared for that."

"Great. I'm here to help, but I am delighted to turn the project into your capable hands."

"You got it. Ship me those files and I'll call if I have questions."

"Great. Thank you."

Tuesday - 4 days until Sea Stars

Something about having Mackenzie come to rehearsal just felt good to Declan. Buoyed by the feeling, he could consider the lurking backstage disasters without panic. After all, they didn't open until Thursday. The play could fall apart, but maybe his life wouldn't. He smiled, thinking about Aurora's face when he introduced Mackenzie. Maybe now that barracuda would leave him alone.

His good mood persisted. Tuesday's rehearsal was a complete run-through with lights and music, but no costumes. He still saw a lot of problem spots, but it was starting to look like a play. A high school play, but a play nevertheless.

Parade details will be managed by a pro, she thought, and now I can just think about what happens at the end of the parade. Speech, we need a speech, she thought. And somebody to give it. She thought about the possible people to give the Sea Stars Festival speech.

Josiah would love it, but no way. No wet blankets.

Charlie Dakin? He'd be great, was well respected in the community and besides, he was easier to get along with than Josiah. But she could not imagine a world in which Charlie would voluntarily get up and make a speech. She could relate.

She pulled out the envelope file that held her notes and dumped it out on the kitchen table. Who else might make a good speaker?

Oh, and who could judge the window contest?

And who was going to draw for the giveaway?

More details remained to manage than she'd realized. Getting the parade off her plate meant she could see what was left, and there was plenty.

A page fluttered to the floor. Swiping it up, she recognized the faded print of the flyer Estelle had pressed on her at their first meeting in the store. Yes, that too. She squinted at the print, then opened a browser window. A few minutes later, she made a call.

"Magda."

"Mackenzie! Nice to hear from you. Did you get things worked out with Kevin?"

"Yes, thank you. He's a wonder. Now I'm thinking about the end of the parade. We need something to happen when they get to Market Square. Like a speech."

"Isn't that when Santa welcomes everyone to the festival? Ho ho ho and all that?"

Mackenzie grimaced. "I don't see Billy Seymour making a speech. We do need a speech though, to thank our sponsors and volunteers."

"Yeah."

"The Marketing Group should make the speech," Mackenzie said. Figure it out, Magda, she thought. That's you.

Silence reigned. Then Magda said, "You're right. We really do need a speech or fireworks or something. The end of the parade should be the climax not the anticlimax."

"Fireworks?" Mackenzie's stomach sank. "I don't think we can pull off fire-works."

Magda gave a short laugh. "I know. Well, the giveaway draw is a big thing, and we have some recognitions for sure. We're going to have to recognize Josiah." They shared a giggle.

"You should give the speech," Mackenzie said, giving up the hope that Magda would take a hint. "You're the chair."

Magda snorted. "I'm an organizer, not a speech-maker. I don't do speeches."

"I'll write it," Mackenzie promised. "All you have to do is read it." Maybe I'll get Declan to check it out, she thought. There should be perks to having a writer and English teacher in the house.

"I don't like it," Magda complained. "Can we just say I'll do it unless we come up with another person? Somebody has to come to mind."

Mackenzie didn't know who, and besides, Magda was the perfect person. But she agreed, anyway, because at least the position was filled provisionally. "Sure. I'll put you down on my list and I'll get a draft speech to you, uh, sometime before you have to give it. Okay?" Not waiting for assent, she continued. "There's another thing, too, we need to talk about."

"What?"

"Can we just make a time to meet? It's about that flyer Estelle gave me."

"Sure. But whatever you want to do about whatever it is, that's fine with me."

"Okay. I'll just move ahead with that part, then," Mackenzie said. "And write your speech."

"I'm not going to stop looking for another speaker," Magda warned her. "There has to be somebody."

"You'll be great. See you soon." Mackenzie hung up. *Wow, that was me reassuring Magda. Imagine that. Maybe I'm actually improving at this stuff.*

Wednesday - 3 days until Sea Stars

At the final bell on Wednesday, Declan dumped his schoolwork into his bag, scanned the classroom and clicked off the lights. He'd marked papers during lunch because there was no other time, and besides, he was too wired up to eat. Heading briskly toward the auditorium, he could hear the noise level rising. Apparently, the kids were wired, too. It was nearly time for dress rehearsal.

The night before, Pat said to the group, "Remember, tomorrow we're going to do this play like it's a performance. Also remember that this is when it'll likely fall apart."

"Yeah," said Patrice. "Whatever can go wrong will go wrong."

"Correct. And why is that a good thing? Chuck?"

"I dunno. Seems like a bad thing to me."

"This way we have a chance to fix things," another boy said. "It's like figuring out where the dragons are."

Kids scoffed and somebody gave him a push. "Everything's not a video game, you know."

"He's got a point," Pat said. "We don't know what can go wrong, but tomorrow night we can find out. That doesn't mean you don't do your very best. There will be an audience out there, even if it is just your parents." The kids, sobered, shuffled out. He'd stayed to walk out with Pat.

"So it's true then," he said. "Bad dress means a good opening?"

She raised her eyebrows. "Well, it's something they say. Maybe so you don't lose hope when it blows up in front of you."

"Is that what we can expect?"

She smiled at him. "You never did Drama Club, did you? Whatever you don't expect that's what to expect. It'll be fine." She patted his arm. His anxiety must be obvious.

Now he looked for Pat as he walked into the auditorium. Three hours until curtain. She was sitting alone in the front row. He sat beside her.

"How's it going?"

She smiled at him. "It's a mess, of course. But they'll come through."

"You're calm," he noted.

She lifted her mug. "Chamomile tea. I give up caffeine the week of the play. There are jitters enough going around."

He nodded. "Makes sense. What do you need me to do?"

"We've done our work well. Now we just let them do theirs."

"You're so good with them. I missed out by avoiding Drama Club when I was in high school."

She smiled at him. "It's never too late."

"Maybe not," he said, and rose to look across the auditorium.

Was he living vicariously through these kids? He hoped not, but he well remembered his own adolescence, always feeling like he was in the small-town spotlight. Everyone knew he'd lost his father and then his mother, that he was lucky his aunt and uncle had taken him in. Declan at fifteen wouldn't have considered drama club. Why would he want all those people looking at him making a fool of himself? At fifteen, just getting through the school day was enough.

But now, this play was putting him on display, as much as the performers. Everyone would know about Declan Kelly, the writer.

He suddenly remembered watching a pet hermit crab climb out of its borrowed shell, then pull itself out of its own shell-like skin, leaving a crab-shaped exoskeleton on the sand. The new, soft skin exposed by molting made it vulnerable to predation until it hardened into a new shell. Risky, yes, but necessary. Otherwise it would die, squeezed into a too-small carapace.

Dress rehearsal of his first-ever play was stretching him into unfamiliar territory, that was certain.

At least he was an adult. Being grown up was so much easier than being a kid. Everything in his life didn't depend on whether people liked his play. He'd be okay, anyway. For some reason, he thought of Mackenzie.

A shout from stage left pulled him from his musings. "Mr. Kelly! Can you help us?" He grinned at Pat and headed toward the call. For the next while, he was involved in last-minute stage direction, application of duct tape, and troubleshooting mechanical glitches for some time. When he emerged again from backstage, curtain time was drawing close.

He returned to the audience side to see Chuck, characteristically untidy, slumped in a seat in the third row. A scattering of kids wandered, chatting, exclaiming, and gesturing theatrically. In contrast, Chuck was leaden, hands tenting his eyes. Declan slid into the seat next to him.

"Hey," he said.

"Hey, Mr. Kelly," said Chuck.

"What's up?"

Chuck sighed. "I can't do it. Not with my parents here."

"Is that so?" Declan asked with interest.

"My dad," Chuck started, but then stopped.

"Your dad what?" Declan encouraged.

Chuck leaned his elbows to knees and turned to look at Declan. "He fishes, Mr. Kelly. You know?"

Declan did know. Chuck's dad was a working man, tough and traditional. "You don't think he'll like the play?"

"I don't think he's going to like me playacting," Chuck said miserably. "This was all a mistake."

"What was?"

"Me doing this. My mum said go ahead, she'd get Dad on board, but now he's invited tonight, and I don't want to do this in front of him."

"Not sure he's ready for his son the actor, eh?"

Chuck scoffed. "Yeah. Some actor."

"My father fished, too, you know."

Chuck looked up with mild interest.

"And my uncle who raised me, he fished."

"Were you in drama?"

"Worse. I wanted to be a writer." He glanced sideways at Chuck. "My uncle turned out to be more open-minded than I expected. Maybe give your dad a chance."

Chuck sighed. "I just hope he'll give my acting a chance."

Declan felt for the kid, but he needed to pull it together. He clapped him on the shoulder and stood up. "Well, if you do your best, I'm pretty sure it'll work out. A lot of people are counting on you."

"Yeah," Chuck said tiredly, getting up, too.

"Chuck! They need you in make-up!" somebody called from the stage.

Chuck sighed even more deeply. "Makeup! My dad's gonna have a cow."

He headed backstage, shoulders slumped. Declan gazed after him. He had no trouble understanding Chuck's misgivings, and he admired the kid for his guts but he had no more time to think about it. He threaded his way through a thickening cluster of kids, some in costume, to get back to Pat. She'd exchanged her mug for a clipboard. He leaned over her shoulder. "What else do you need me to do?"

She smiled at him. "Not a thing, Mr. Playwright. Tonight you get to sit in the audience and just listen. Take some notes, too, if you see something we need to fix."

"Okay," he agreed. "That sounds easy."

"I appreciate everything you've done, Dec, including that little intervention with Chuck there," Pat said quietly. "He's come a long way, but acting in front of his father requires a leap of faith."

"So he said."

She looked at her watch. "Time, everybody! Curtain in thirty minutes." Then she looked back at Declan. "Sorry. I was wrong. You can't just sit down, at least not yet. Could you please keep the audience outside until five minutes before curtain?" She grinned at him. "Then, I promise, you get to sit and watch."

"Sure," he said. "I'll fight them tooth and nail to keep out of the auditorium."

She nodded toward the back. "You better start now. I think that's Jodie's grandmother trying to get in."

It was close to midnight when he finally slipped into bed beside Mackenzie after eating leftovers while standing in front of the fridge, checking the pellet stove, and locking the doors as usual.

"How was it?" she asked sleepily.

"Awful," he said with satisfaction. "One set fell down, three kids flubbed lines, the team running the lights and sound lost the only copy of the script that they'd kept notes on, so they had to make a new one as they went. It was terrible."

She giggled. "You sound happy. What gives?"

"Bad dress means a good first night, or so they say," he said. "There's a lot of fixing and back-filling and just plain work to be done before seven p.m. tomorrow."

"Hmm." She snuggled into him.

"I'm happy to report it isn't my work to do," he murmured, sleepy. "Oh, and Chuck Thibodeau's dad didn't show up."

"Untucked Chuck?"

"The very same. He's scared of his dad seeing him in makeup and playacting, but dad didn't come."

"Is that a good thing or not?"

Declan made a noise. "No idea. Chuck did well, but it was only his mother and his three aunties."

"Lucky Chuck."

"Maybe." Declan was unsure.

"I just mean to have so many people come," Mackenzie said. "And you care about him, too."

He pulled her a little closer. "I care about you." It was easy to forget Mackenzie had grown up with almost nobody in her life, only a mother who kept her away from other people. He couldn't imagine how this lovable woman had been so unloved.

"Mmmm," she murmured into his shoulder.

He breathed in her fragrance, settled into her warmth, and sank promptly into a deep sleep.

Part IV

Thursday - 2 days until Sea Stars

Mackenzie bought tickets for all three shows. Declan had warned her the shows would likely sell out, since the auditorium was small and everybody in town would be there at least once. On Thursday, she called Kathy to invite her.

"Jake and I are already going tonight," her sister said. "The twins reserved Saturday for themselves and requested that their parents not be present."

"What?" Mackenzie laughed.

"Seems fair enough to me," Kathy said. "There are girls involved and they didn't want their parents along on their date. Besides, I only need to go once."

"Well, I probably only need to go once, too, but if I want to see my partner this week, I have to go to the play, because that's where he'll be."

"Not easy, is it?" Kathy said thoughtfully.

"Not terrible," Mackenzie said, not wanting to complain. "I'm busy, too. By the way, did we get Christmas dinner sorted?"

Kathy laughed out loud. "Sorted? You volunteered, that's the way I remember it."

"We did. I didn't know if you all were okay with that," Mackenzie said diffidently. "I know you always do Christmas dinner."

"By default. Not because it's my favourite thing to do. I just had the most kids, so I did the inviting. I'm more than happy to let you take over."

"I'm not taking over," Mackenzie demurred. "Let me give it a shot this year and then we can assess. I might burn the turkey or something worse."

"No pie. That would be worse."

"Okay, maybe that." Mackenzie started to think about all the things that could go wrong. "Maybe I was premature in taking this on."

Kathy laughed again. "No way, sis, you are not getting out of this."

Mackenzie was quiet.

"Mack? I'll help. It's just a meal, not a production. No perfection required."

She let out her breath. "I just panicked there for a minute."

"No panic. If you haven't cooked for a crowd before, it can be daunting. But we'll do it together, okay?"

"Okay."

"Just at your house," Kathy said, chortling again. "Listen, I'll send you my notes from last year."

"Notes? You have notes?" Mackenzie felt the panic rise again. "I thought you said it was just a meal."

"Well, yes. But there are some things to keep in mind." Kathy laughed. "I'll help, I promise. You can put Declan to work."

Right, Mackenzie thought, if he ever comes home. She stopped that thought immediately. Things were better. They were both making them better.

"Okay," she said a little unsteadily. "We can do this."

"You bet we can," Kathy said enthusiastically. "At your house."

On opening night, Declan felt flutters, but the noise in the auditorium suggest-ed the kids' flutters were a lot bigger. They were certainly loud. Pat was calm, fielding last minute questions and crises. Dec sat in the dark of the back row, gazing down at the stage.

He glanced to his left as Mackenzie eased in next to him. "Hi," she said, slipping her coat off her shoulders. "Is this where we're sitting? The back row?"

He caught his breath at the sight of her. Her brown eyes were deep, even darker than usual, her hair swept up in a twist. The creamy sheath dress looked made for her. He recognized the earrings he'd given her for her last birthday. She smelled great, too. He leaned over to kiss her cheek. "You are so beautiful," he said, smiling.

"Thank you."

"We're sitting here because the sound is best here, and you can slip out if someone needs you in a hurry. I mean, I can slip out if I have to."

"I guess that's a teacher thing," she said. "I was thinking of this more as coming to the theatre."

"That's right, that's how we want it to be," he said. "But yes, I am a teacher first, playwright second."

"Okay, then, teacher-playwright. I'm looking forward to seeing your cre-ation."

He kissed her for real then, in the semi-darkness of the back row, taking enough time to feel her soften against his chest. "I'm so glad you're here. It wouldn't be the same without you," he said. "I do have to check on the ticket takers, though, because last I heard Mrs. Grundy wasn't coming."

She stood to let him up, and he turned to face her as he crab-walked by, their faces so close that he brushed her lips with his. "I'll be right back," he said. "I hope."

Mackenzie had low expectations after the snippets she'd seen on Monday, but knew things could improve. She liked the script, but would she like the play? If anyone asked her opinion, she wanted to be wholehearted in her appreciation.

She sat, hands folded in her lap, while the audience filtered in and the buzz of excitement built. This was it. The culmination of all Declan's work. The long summer evenings of writing, fall revisions, readings, auditions and rehearsals had come to this point. Fruition. Completion. Realization of a dream, really. The Drama Club kids had no idea how important this play was.

Or maybe they did. They were lucky, she thought, to have Pat and Declan working for them, with them.

Declan was missing, though, and she found her hands twisting together. She consciously let them relax into her lap as he slid into his seat the same moment one of the kids got up to make the land acknowledgement. Mackenzie listened carefully to her words about the "traditional, unceded territory of the Mi'kmaq, Woolostaquey, and Peskotomuhkati people," the First Nations peoples whose stories of Glooscap had been new to her. Then the curtain swept up to enthusiastic applause.

Declan held her hand throughout the first act, then he had to leave again during the brief intermission. He didn't get back until the middle of Act Two, but by that time Mackenzie was so absorbed in the story, she barely noticed his absence until intermission. As the lights came up, she stood to stretch, and walked down the auditorium aisle.

"Mackenzie!" She looked around to see Magda waving to her from a seat. She walked over.

"Hi, Magda," she said. Magda stood. "This is my partner, Jesse," she said. "And where's your man?"

"He's being a teacher, I guess," Mackenzie said. "Did you know this is his play?"

"What do you mean?" Magda asked. "Is he the drama club adviser?"

"Well, he helps out, but he wrote the play."

"Really? It's pretty brilliant. I love the local colour as well as the hero theme. Maybe I'll get to meet him tonight."

"I'd like for you to meet him," Mackenzie said, looking around again. "Hopefully we'll see you after the show."

Maybe he was here somewhere in the audience. Oh, there he was, leaning against the wall of the auditorium near the back. Aurora Smithers had her hand on the wall by his shoulder, head leaned toward his. Mackenzie narrowed her eyes. "I'll see you later," she said to Magda, and headed through the throng toward Declan. Before she'd taken two steps, though, the lights flickered, and people started back to their seats.

She met Declan at their seats in the back row. "Hey," she said. "I wanted you to meet Magda, my sometimes boss, sometimes friend. She's impressed with your play."

"Sure," he said, smiling down at her. "I'd like to meet your friends."

"I saw Aurora holding you hostage. I was coming to your rescue, but the lights went down."

He shook his head. "She doesn't quit. I might have to complain."

"Maybe," she agreed. "Oh, look, it's starting."

The curtain opened on the third act, Patrice intoning lines as the Queen of Fundy. Mackenzie looked at Declan's profile, his gaze intense at the stage. Was he whispering the dialogue? Well, mouthing it, at least. She settled back into her seat.

The unnamed boy from the village had braved the whirlpool, diving directly into the Old Sow that threatened to drown the village. Collapsing into a heap, he woke in a forest of kelp, a bunch of kids in dark green costumes, chanting, "Into the deep. Into the deep."

"Old Sow is a real whirlpool," Declan murmured. "That's a change to the script."

Makenzie nodded and kept watching the stage.

Shaking himself off, the boy stepped outside the kelp forest into the court of the King and Queen of the Bay of Fundy. The members of the court sported mermaid tails and lots of colours and sequins. Patrice, swathed in white tulle, and her consort, the King, announced the capture of yet another boatful of fishers. The boy approached, hesitant, frightened yet determined.

"The village sent me to ask for the return of our people. We need their wisdom to help us convince the Old Sow not to drown our village."

The King was adamant. "Your kind! You trample on the earth, on the sea. You dump pollution into our Bay."

The Queen weighed in, too. "You harm animals of the land and the sea. The Bay is warming. The whales are leaving. We would be better off without you."

"Let the Old Sow drown you in her whirlpool!" the King shouted and raised his sceptre, accompanied by loud noises and darkness cut by flashing lights. Scenes from the Bay of Fundy were shown on a screen above the stage with loud narration by the royal couple.

Shocked and terrified, the boy fell to the floor. Soon the court became quiet. Light returned to normal.

"I didn't know," he said to the court. "I didn't know about all that damage." The kelp forest took up the chant. "He didn't know. He didn't know." It rose to a peak, then trailed off.

"How could you be so ignorant?" demanded the Queen. "You knew your people were lost. Did you have no thoughts for other lives?"

"I knew it wasn't safe for our people. I didn't know we made it unsafe for you."

The King waved his sceptre again and darkness and flashing lights spread across the stage. "You claim ignorance, but you did harm! Much harm! Reparation is required."

After a moment, the boy could be heard. "We can change! Let us know how to change. I will see that our village changes our practices."

"Changing now won't bring back the whales. You cannot undo the harm you have done." There was more banging and darkness.

The boy entreated the royals. "Tell me how we can work together. Tell me what we can do."

The King and Queen gazed at each other. The boy continued, "Give back our people. They hold the old wisdom. We need them."

The kelp forest chanted, "Back from the dead. Back from the dead."

The King approached the boy. "I can't do that. Nobody can do that. We don't control Nature."

"Can nobody help me?"

The queen weighed in. "You want to go against Nature, to bring the dead back to life. Fighting Nature makes things harder for life itself. We are not your enemy."

The kelp forest chanted again. "We are not your enemy. We are not your enemy."

After awhile, the chanting quieted and the boy asked, "Is Nature my enemy?"

The Queen scoffed. "What are you if not an expression of Nature? Your kind is like a wilful child, fighting against the one who gave you life."

"My parents gave me life. Fishing is how they feed me and my kind. We need them back."

"They mean nothing to us," Queen responded. "They are here because they died. They did not respect the Nature of the Bay, of the storms and tides and whirlpools that become dangerous when you try to breach them."

"I cannot restore the dead to life, my young visitor," the King said kindly. "I cannot change what your kind is doing to your own nature. But you can."

"I can what? I can't restore life," the boy said sharply.

"What can he do? What can he do? What can he do?" the forest of kelp sang. The boy fell back to sleep while the King and Queen slid quietly offstage and the stage lights dimmed.

From behind the scenes came a strong woman's voice. "You cannot restore life. But you can protect it."

Mackenzie was rapt. What would happen next? She noticed Declan glancing her way and leaned into him a little. But her gaze stayed on the stage. The woman's voice went on with more insights, then faded into a musical interlude as the scene shifted.

The kelp forest shucked their dark green to reveal the lighter green of trees. They chanted quietly while making a half circle around the boy, who lay asleep in the village. The chant changed from "What can he do?" to "do what you can do, do what you can do…"

Gradually, the sun rose and the villagers gathered. The chant faded away, trees quiet in the presence of humans.

"He's wet," someone observed.

"He's been in the Bay. Went down the Old Sow," said an old lady in the crowd.

"Nobody goes into the Old Sow."

"The Old Sow wants to kill us."

"Old Sow? Nobody comes back from there," someone else said.

"Call the doctor. He went into the Old Sow."

The doctor came and stated, "Nobody survives the Old Sow."

"I did," the boy said. He sat up. "I came back."

"What did you find?" someone asked.

"The sea is full of mysteries," he said, standing. "I am full of mysteries."

"Did you find them? Our villagers?"

"There is no mystery there," he said. "They died in the Bay."

There was a general uproar.

The boy went on. "We miss them and wish they were here. But they are dead."

More crying came from the crowd. The forest chanted, "We are not dead. But we will die." The chanting increased in volume and speed, while a villager pounded a rhythmic drumbeat.

After increasing in intensity for some time, the chanting slowed and quieted.

The auditorium was profoundly silent. On the stage, an old lady emerged from the crowd of villagers.

"Everyone will die," she said.

"Some of us sooner than others," said another lady from the crowd on stage. She vamped a little and got a snicker from the audience. "That's not news."

Villagers took turns speaking.

"Despair says, if we are going to die, why even try to make the world better?"

"We tried to make a better world," said another. "We failed. We poisoned the waters, warmed the air so the glaciers are melting, killed off whole species of animal, made the world safer for viruses to harm us."

"Right," agreed another villager.

"In our quest to help, we often harmed."

"Despair, despair, despair," the forest chanted into a crescendo along with the drum, then subsiding.

Silence fell again as the lighting shifted. Not breathing, Mackenzie waited to see what would happen.

"It is not all failure," said the boy. "Life moves to the next generation." The young villagers gathered together on one side of the stage with the older ones on the opposite side. The boy, in the middle, continued, "Life goes on. Where did you succeed?"

The forest started to chant again and the projected images of the King and Queen appeared above the villagers. It was clear only the boy could see them.

The older villagers shouted out lines and the boy repeated them to the King and Queen.

"We changed the shipping lanes to protect the whales," said one.

"We stopped overfishing," said another.

"We learned about sustainable farming."

After a few more examples, the villagers grew quiet. The boy looked up at the images of the royal couple and said, "All is not failure."

"All is not failure," the King agreed, and their images faded to black.

The boy climbed onto a fallen tree trunk and the villagers, old and young, gathered to listen. "We will protect that which is ours to protect."

"Will that bring our people back? Or keep us safe in the Bay next week?"

"No. Personal death is inevitable, but protection for our home, our land and water and air, will carry on."

"Yes!" the villagers shouted. "We will protect what we can protect."

The forest began a new chant, building in volume. "Protect our water, protect our land, protect our air, protect our life."

The villagers gathered around the boy. The chanting ended, and he stated, "This is the wisdom I learned in the Old Sow."

The strong female voice spoke again as the scene darkened. "This is the wisdom of the ancestors, and the wisdom of the land and sea."

The silence in the auditorium was profound. The curtain dropped and the place exploded with applause and cheers, and people standing and whistling. Mackenzie's eyes were damp as she clapped and clapped, standing along with the rest of the audience.

"Who was that kid?" she asked Declan. "I didn't get a program."

He looked at her with shiny eyes. "That was Chuck. Our very own Chuck."

Touched by his emotion, she leaned into his arm. "It was beautiful. He was great."

She wasn't surprised by the standing ovation, not only because the audience members were family and friends, but the play was that good. That touching. Declan, jubilant, cheered from the back row, and Mackenzie cheered, too. The kids took an awkward group bow, and the curtain closed for the last time. The audience settled, and people started to gather their things and leave.

"It was wonderful," she said sincerely. "I'm so proud of you. The story came across, and the kids really did it justice."

"Thanks. It was good, wasn't it? The kids did well." Declan gave her a tight hug.

"Not just the kids. It was your ideas, come to life. Wonderful."

He held her off to look at her. "It's a little hard to take in," he said, eyes glistening again.

"Get used to it," she advised. "A lot of people are going to want to talk to you." She smiled at him.

"Yeah, maybe." He looked around, gathering himself. "I've got to, uh, check in down there," he said, gesturing toward the stage. "I'll see you at home."

"You're not coming now?" she asked, surprised.

"Do you want to wait? I won't be too long."

She considered. "We've got two cars anyway," she finally said. "No, you go ahead. Soak up the congratulations. The whole evening was magical, really."

He gave her a big smile, held her by the shoulders and briskly kissed her, then headed down the aisle against the flow of traffic. She watched him being stopped by one person and another, congratulations flowing, she was sure. He looked happy.

Carrying her coat over her arm, she headed for the lobby. Kathy and Jake were by the outside doors. "Hi," she said. She wiped a little tear.

"Yup, it got me, too," Kathy said. "Who knew Declan had all that in him? By the way, you look great. That dress suits you. Dad would have said you look like a million bucks."

"Thanks," she said.

"Where is Dec?" asked Jake, looking behind her. "All those lost fishermen got me right in the feels, as they used to say."

"It was really something," Kathy agreed. "When you think how his father died, you know."

Mackenzie's eyes smarted. "It was beautiful," she choked out. "Especially that boy, the one who tries to save the village?"

Kathy patted her on the shoulder. "He did a great job," she said. "That kid but also Declan."

"Yeah," Mackenzie said. "He's busy getting congratulations," she said, rummaging for a tissue.

"Well deserved," Jake said. "I've read some of his short stories, but this was entirely different. Not what I expected, but great."

"I thought he'd be with you," Kathy noted.

"He was. We sat together, but we've got separate cars, so I'm heading home. Unless you want to catch him at the stage door." She gestured down the hall to where a cluster of adults and teens hovered, some holding flowers. She didn't want Kathy worrying about her relationship with Declan.

A sudden surge of activity happened there, as the door burst open and a bunch of kids emerged, most still wearing stage makeup.

"Funny how much bigger they look onstage," Kathy said.

Pat MacRae came out behind the kids and was immediately accosted by parents.

"It looks pretty busy there," Jake said. "I'll give him a call later. Come on, Kath."

"It is late for us old folks," Kathy said with a smile. "See you later."

"Bye, Mackenzie," Jake added.

Mackenzie said, "I'll walk out with you." She did miss Declan, but she was tired. She accompanied Kathy and Jake to the parking lot.

"Well done," Declan said to Chuck as the crowds thinned in the hallway. "What did you think?"

"Okay. I didn't mess up my lines this time."

"You sure didn't. Did you hear all that applause when you dove into the Old Sow? And again at the end?"

Chuck looked bemused. "Not really. I was kind of busy."

Declan laughed. "Well, that's probably good. What did your father say?"

"Not here." The boy shook his head. "Not tonight. Mum was here, though. She liked it."

"You did great, Chuck."

"Yeah, I guess. Good enough, anyway."

"Chuck. Not just good enough. Very well done."

Chuck shrugged. "Okay."

"Maybe your dad will come tomorrow. Or Saturday."

"Maybe." He walked down the corridor, head down. Declan looked after him, bemused. The approval of his teachers and his mom were just not enough. That boy really needed his father. Declan sighed and headed for the door.

By the time he got to the parking lot, his own excitement and pleasure in the evening resurfaced. He hummed to himself as he headed to his pickup in the far reaches of the nearly empty lot. The half-moon was faded by mist at the top of a gnarled, naked oak. Scudding clouds darkened the night sky further. Leaning against his truck, he heard the distant sounds of laughter and car doors slamming as people left the school. The December quiet closed around him.

It had been a good night. The play was okay, better than okay, and it had been well-received. Warm inside from the evening, he recalled congratulations, and the sweetness of Mackenzie next to him.

He gazed toward the twisted silhouette of a lone oak tree. It had marked the end of school property since he'd been a student. Phys ed classes raced to the tree and back, kids were rousted out for smoking behind it, and he'd once asked a girl for a date while standing under it. It was as old as the school, maybe as old as the village. He wondered about all the things that tree had seen, all the Declans it had witnessed, his gangly fourteen-year-old self, the eighteen-year-old trying to fit in, and his return to Stella Mare, not the triumphant swagger of a successful novelist. He could still be that, of course, but for right now, he was a teacher, one who leads young people. And tonight, a playwright watching his work in performance.

He let out a sigh of satisfaction.

Satisfaction—that feeling-was amplified because of sharing it with Mackenzie. He didn't understand how another person could make you feel more like yourself, but she did. She gave him more reasons to keep working, keep striving, now that he knew there was someone he could make a life with. Minor success as a high-school teacher-and-playwright meant so much more because she was with him. She was part of it.

Suddenly, he couldn't wait to get home to her.

Friday - 1 day until Sea Stars

Mackenzie and Declan were up early as usual.

"You're coming again tonight?" He stopped pouring coffee to look at her. "Really?"

"Really." she said. "I wouldn't miss it."

He turned back to filling his travel mug, feeling something wash over him. His eyes smarted with tears, for some reason. Capping the mug, he sat across from her. "That's really above and beyond. I can't tell you how much I appreciate it." He wasn't sure he liked this exposure, all his feelings right on his face.

"It's what we do, right?" She smiled as she looked into his eyes. He felt a quick stab of regret for the nights he let her go to bed alone. That was going to change. Immediately.

"We try," he agreed. "Are you frantic with the festival tomorrow?"

"There's only so much more I can do," she said. "Besides, the play is an event. I'm the only person in town whose boyfriend's play is being performed at the local high school."

He laughed at that. "So true."

"Besides, then I'll get to see Aurora Smithers in action again."

He sighed. "She's something, isn't she? I think I've been clear, but she keeps pushing."

"In some places, you'd call that sexual harassment," Mackenzie said.

"Oh, I don't know," he demurred. "Annoying, yes, but I don't know if it's harassment."

"It would be if the genders were reversed. It's easier to see when you think of that. Imagine if I had a boss who kept asking me out."

"Yes, that's obvious. It seems more complicated for men, maybe. I do think she'll give it up. It's not going anywhere, that's for sure."

"It doesn't hurt for me to be visible," she said. "We're a team, right?"

He reached across the table for her hand. "We are totally a team."

Giving her fingers a squeeze, he turned to pull on his jacket, heft his backpack, and head for the door. Glancing back, he saw those warm brown eyes above her sweet smile.

"I love you so much, Mackenzie Brown," he said, then was out the door into the cold damp December morning.

Mackenzie had great expectations after the wonderful opening night, but Friday's performance was plagued with problems. Some disaster happened early that called Declan backstage before the opening curtain and he never returned to his seat. Mackenzie didn't mind watching on her own, but she worried for the kids and for Dec. The sparkle was missing, and flubbed lines, missed entrances and a major malfunction with the curtain either reflected, or contributed to, an uneven performance. While not terrible, it wasn't up to the previous night's standards. The audience was enthusiastic regardless. That's the benefit of being in a small town where everyone is family or friends, she thought.

Declan looked tired when she caught up with him backstage. He gave her a distracted hug as he continued to talk with the drama kids, keeping his arm across her shoulders.

"There were a couple of problems, right, you guys? Do you know what they were?"

"Yeah, Chuck messed up," somebody said.

"Not only," Chuck said. "I mean, yeah, I did, but…"

"He's right, I did too. Missed my cue."

"Right. A few mistakes. Then that compounded because you let it rattle you." Declan's voice was calm, measured.

"It felt like it was falling apart." A girl sniffled.

"It didn't fall apart, though. It just felt that way, but you recovered. Take a little time to think about what you need to do differently. We all want a great closing night."

"I'm gonna be up all night," a girl said. "No more mistakes."

Declan shook his head. "No, don't do that. Get sleep. Eat. Rest. You have all worked hard, you all know what you're doing. Don't focus on what was wrong. Visualize how you want to do it."

Pat MacRae looked up from the notes she was scribbling. "Mr. Kelly is right. We don't focus on mistakes. Let's think about what you did well. What did we do right?" she asked.

The group was silent. Then somebody giggled. "You mean just like in the play."

"Right," Pat said. "It works. What did we do well?"

"Well, we started on time."

"Yes. And what else?"

Soon the kids were spilling over with comments about what had gone well, and the mood lightened considerably. Mackenzie gazed at her guy and these kids. Something palpable was happening here. Some bit of uplift, maybe, or perhaps this was just what support looked like.

"Okay, guys, time to turn in," Declan said. In the general din, Pat talked to a couple of kids, and Declan and Mackenzie started to ease away.

"Hey, is that your wife?" a boy asked.

Declan pulled her closer. "This is Mackenzie, you guys."

"I didn't know he was married," a girl said somewhere behind Mackenzie.

"He's not," someone else said. "She's just his girlfriend."

"She's prettier than Ms. Smithers."

"Eeew! Ms. Smithers is too old. Come on."

"Mr. Kelly is old, too."

Mackenzie heard that exchange loud and clear, though she was pretty sure Declan missed it while listening to something else. It was inevitable that adolescent girls would have some opinions about their teachers, especially their recently-single handsome teachers. She wondered if she passed muster with the girls in the drama club. "Just" his girlfriend indeed.

"Let's go," Declan said into her ear. "I'm beat."

They climbed into bed together, cuddling for warmth while Murphy snored on the floor. "This is nice," she said.

"Umm," he mumbled, face in her neck.

"Are you agreeing with me? I didn't get it." She giggled.

Turning his head so she could hear, he said "I want more of this kind of time with you."

"Good idea. Can I tell you something?"

"Of course. Tell away."

"I liked what you said to the kids about not dwelling on the mistakes."

"Yeah? It wasn't original, you know."

"Yeah, you got it from your play," she giggled. "That's not important. What's important is how you used it. It might have been the first time any of them ever heard it applied to them. I feel like it was the first time for me, even though it probably wasn't. I grew up focused on mistakes. I was a mistake my mother made. She was always looking for mistakes. Her own and others'. Mine." Her chest was tight.

He leaned up on an elbow, looking into her face. Tiny fatigue lines framed his eyes, but their dark blue looked deep into her. She felt his attention softening her heart.

He traced her cheek with a finger. "It's hard to move forward when you beat yourself up for the past," he said. "All your energy goes to trying to survive."

"Trying not to make another mistake. Trying not to BE a mistake."

"You're the best thing that ever showed up in my life," he said. "You are not a mistake."

A tear slid down her cheek. "It's not easy for me to remember that. I get so scared of doing something wrong. Mistakes feel like the end of everything."

"I guess they can be, if you're out in a fishing boat in a storm," he said, "but mostly, everyday mistakes are just opportunities to learn to do things better."

"I love how you talk to the kids," she said. "I know you're a writer first, but you seem to be a natural teacher. You're a good person for these kids to learn from. What you're doing at the high school, that's important work." She gazed at him, willing him to understand.

He was quiet, too. "I get more from the kids then they get from me," he said finally. "When they try hard and finally succeed, I feel it myself. When they try and fail, I can help them because I've been there. Teaching has turned out to be a bigger thing than I expected. I don't mean more work. Just maybe, well, more important."

"Well, you're needed there. Just like you're needed here." She tugged, pulling his face to hers. "For all sorts of reasons."

Some time later, Mackenzie watched the moonlight travel across the old plaster wall, while Declan snored peacefully beside her. Her mind was awash with lists, images, and memories, and she didn't notice when she slipped into sleep. Her mother appeared in a fitful dream, but then changed into Magda and, finally, Estelle. She awoke with a start, relieved to find it was still hours before morning. The festival hadn't yet begun.

She hoped she'd thought of everything but was sure she hadn't. Besides, she reasoned, nothing ever goes off without a hitch. She could only try to anticipate the problems and hope for the grace and aplomb of Declan and Pat, but there was no dress rehearsal for a village festival.

Part V

Saturday - The Sea Stars Festival

Getting up before the sun wasn't hard at winter solstice. Despite her poor sleep, Mackenzie rose before five, her mind racing. When Declan came downstairs at seven, she was hard at work. He leaned over her shoulder and kissed her cheek, rubbing his stubbly cheek against her. She reached up absently to pat his other cheek but was absorbed in the screen in front of her. She'd been fielding text messages since six. He dropped a kiss on her head and turned toward the coffeemaker.

"I keep finding loose ends," she announced. "I don't have anybody assigned to pick the giveaway winner."

"Hm," he said, sitting across from her.

"I'm not even sure we've got a system to get all the entries in the same place," she muttered, scrolling her notes. "Uh oh."

"Mackenzie," he said.

Frowning at her spreadsheet, she barely heard him.

"Listen to me," he said. "I can do that. Really. I'm available to help today."

"No, you can't," she said, not looking up. "It has to happen after four p.m, but before five. You'll be at school."

"Oh, right," he said, looking away. "Sorry about that."

She looked up then. "No need for sorry. I should have planned better. Maybe I can do it."

He shook his head. "Delegate. That's a task to delegate."

"Yeah, it's just that everyone is going to be busy with the parade at that time. Oh, wait." She tapped away. "Maybe Magda can do it. It'll keep her mind off having to give a speech. When she meets the parade at Market Square, Santa can pull the winner." She looked up with a tired smile. "Thanks."

He scoffed at that. "Okay, I did absolutely nothing. That was entirely you."

"You help me think," she said. "Sometimes."

He snickered. "I bet you haven't eaten anything. Can I make you breakfast?"

After pancakes Mackenzie could hardly choke down, they headed downtown in two vehicles, Murphy opting for Mackenzie's Corolla. Mackenzie planned to check in with the participating businesses, and Declan ready to be deployed where needed. They were standing outside Dakin's Hardware when her phone rang.

"Oh, hi, Estelle," she said, giving Declan a puzzled glance.

"This food has to go now," Estelle said firmly. "All these boxes are taking up a lot of space."

"It's going to St. James Church. Can't Josiah take it?"

"He's off gallivanting with some float or other," Estelle snapped. "Could you come get it?"

Mackenzie raised her eyebrows at Declan. "Yes, of course. We have a volunteer with a truck who will come by in just a few minutes. Are you sure you don't want to keep the collection going today? It should be busy."

"The boxes are a fire hazard here. They have to go right away."

"It sounds like there's a lot of food," Mackenzie said. "That's good. We can help more people."

"Just have your truck guy come get it out of here."

Apparently Estelle was not in the mood for congratulations on the success of the food drive. "Sure. Will do," she said, looking at Declan. "Thank you, Estelle." She hung up.

"Can you pick up the donations at the Save Mart and take them to the church? Estelle is tired of having them clutter up the store, I guess."

"Sure. That's what I signed on for today," Declan said with great cheer. "Shall we say hello to Charlie Dakin first?" He nodded toward the hardware store.

"Sure. Estelle can wait another ten minutes. Dakin's was my destination, anyway."

The hardware store was busy. Mackenzie sidled up to Charlie after he finished with a customer. "Everything okay?" she asked.

He nodded. "Hey, you two. Nice to see you together. Yep, everything's going fine. This festival might have been a good idea after all." He smiled down at Mackenzie and gave her a nod before turning to the next customer.

"Wonderful," she said with relief, then followed Declan to the door.

"That was easy," Declan said.

"Charlie turned out to be a supporter," she said, looking through the store window at the line of customers snaking through the aisle. "I underestimated him."

"Looks like a good start to the day," Declan observed. "I better head over to the Save Mart."

"Yes, please," Mackenzie said. "I know we can't please everyone, but I don't want Estelle mad at me."

He looked askance. "Why Estelle?"

Abashed, she said, "Okay, anyone. I don't want anyone mad at me."

He chuckled. "It's all going to be fine. Charlie is as happy as a pig in clover."

"What? A what?"

"Never mind." He bumped her with his shoulder and grinned. "It's just a thing they say. I'm going now."

Mackenzie continued her check-in with the downtown businesses after Declan drove off toward the Save Mart. She was pleased to see most stores were decorated, customers were filing in, and Market Square already had several food trucks and restaurant booths set up. Things looked good. The gulls were hyperactive with the appearance of food near the wharf. She could relate to their excitement.

"Hey, Mackenzie," a harsh voice called from Jessie's Pizza, halfway down the square.

She walked toward the speaker swathed in a big white apron on the front deck. "Make sure them trucks don't park in front of my place, now."

"Hi, Tracey," Mackenzie said, keeping a pleasant expression. "They won't. Everybody has an assigned place. Do you want to see the map?"

"Nah, that's okay. You just keep an eye out."

"Sure," Mackenzie said, waving at her and heading back up to Water Street. Sure, she could monitor the food trucks. Sure, she could move the food to the church. What other unrealistic expectations would people have for her? She tried, unsuccessfully, to take a deep breath. Instead, her phone rang again.

"Mackenzie? Magda here. Are you crazy already?"

"Not quite yet. But I'm so happy to hear from you." She spoke rapidly, as if Magda might hang up before she could get it all out. "Can you pick up the giveaway entries after four but before five? Also, it sounds like we need somebody to help the food trucks find their spots so they don't cut off the restaurants. I thought people could read a map but I was wrong. I already had to send Declan to pick up the food collection because Estelle's annoyed."

"Breathe!" Magda said with a laugh. "Take a breath. There's nothing life or death happening here."

"I'm trying," she said. "I thought I had it all figured out."

"You did," Magda said. "You do. Mostly. Yes, of course I'll pick up the giveaway entries. No problem."

"Are you sure you can fit it in? You've got to pick up the Santa costume in St Stephen." And give a big speech, she thought, but didn't say aloud.

"Oh, there's plenty of time. I can't get the costume until one p.m. because it's being used in another parade this morning. I'll drop it off at the assembly place for the parade around three thirty, then go get the giveaway entries. It's a little village. It'll be fine."

Mackenzie was thinking furiously. "Okay. Thank you. As long as we have the entries at Market Square before the parade arrives, we're golden."

"Who's doing the draw, anyway?"

The bottom dropped out of Mackenzie's stomach. "We agreed on Santa. Right?"

"Yeah, only…" Magda gave a nervous giggle.

"What?"

"Well, I heard Billy Seymour was stuffing the giveaway boxes at the Sunshine Diner. What if he picks himself?"

Mackenzie had to laugh. "Okay, we need somebody other than Billy. Someone who won't have an entry in the draw. You could do it."

"Not a chance," Magda said. "I'm already in the spotlight too much. We'll figure it out. A festival is for fun, right?"

"You'll have to convince me," Mackenzie said darkly, but she giggled.

Once she'd visited the last business, she drove to Saint James Church to check on the pie café and cookie sale. Everything seemed to be going well there, including the last-minute float construction happening in the back parking lot, where Josiah waved his arms, calling out instructions. After glancing at the group, she walked back to the front. She didn't need to have a conversation with Josiah.

As she walked across the parking lot, Declan's truck pulled up beside her.

"Hey, good-looking. Want a ride in my truck?" He leered at her.

"Funny guy. Next you'll be offering me candy."

"Well, I'm glad to see you," he said.

"You don't look glad. I'd call that a worried look. How's it going?"

"Okay, I guess, except Josiah was mad that I brought the food over."

"What? Estelle demanded that we get it out of the store."

"I guess she didn't tell him. He was expecting you'd be making a big publicity thing out of getting the donations from the Save Mart, no doubt with Josiah as the saviour of Stella Mare."

Mackenzie snorted. "I just saw him out back. He seemed happy enough ordering folks around on the float committee."

"Well, I might have intervened," he said, a little abashed. "I told him you planned a public acknowledgement and photo op when the parade reaches Market Square. I hope that's okay."

She pulled out her phone to make a note. "We'll make it okay. Good solution. So that's something to add to the speech. The speech that Magda still thinks we can hand off to some unknown person."

"Your opportunity lies ahead," he said with a grin.

She scoffed. "Yeah. What are you, a magic eight-ball?"

"I aim to please."

"Maybe Santa will do it," she said. "I have high hopes for Santa. Where are you headed now?"

"Somebody asked me to move some furniture that was donated to the rummage sale. Do you need me?"

"Always," she said with a smile. "But right now, you're doing good work right there. Thanks for your help." She leaned into the cab for a quick kiss.

"Love you," he said with a wink and a smile before driving off. With a sigh, she headed behind the church to straighten things out with Josiah.

By one p.m., she was in dire need of some quiet time. She escaped busy Water Street to drive down Fish House Road. Parking the Corolla on the side of the gravel track, she took a deep breath for the first time all day. The air off the water was still crisply cold, but inside her car she was warm and toasty. Sunshine poured across the dash, and the blanket from the backseat added a layer of warmth. Murphy moaned with pleasure and settled deeper in the backseat. Her head lolled and she closed her eyes.

Her phone woke her and the dog.

"Hi, Magda." She tried to sound alert.

"Hi. We've got a problem."

She closed her eyes, then opened them. "Okay. Tell me."

"There's no Santa costume."

"They said it would be there by one p.m."

"Yeah, well, it's here. It's just that it got peed on at the morning event and there's no time to clean it."

"What? They must be used to that," Mackenzie said, heart in her throat. "Can't they clean it? We have to have a Santa costume."

"I don't know what to tell you. I've seen it and smelled it. It can't be used, probably ever again. The costume store tried every place they knew of to get an alternate, but we are just out of luck."

Mackenzie slumped over the steering wheel, holding her head. "Oh, no. This is the worst. We can't have a Santa without the suit." No Santa, unhappy children, unhappy parents, no fun at all. It would ruin the festival, at least for the kids. Murphy whined from the backseat.

"I'm so sorry," Magda said. "I hate bringing bad news."

"It's not your fault, obviously." She sat up and gazed past the old fish houses at the grey water, fishing boats floating on their moorings. The nearest boat sported a Christmas wreath. "I might have an idea. What does a Maritime Santa wear? Could there be a Santa who doesn't wear a fuzzy red suit?"

"What are you thinking?"

"What does the Santa of the Sea wear?" She put Magda on speaker and started scrolling her phone.

"Santa of the Sea? You're ahead of me, Mackenzie."

"Maybe the Sea Stars Santa wears hauling gear, like those yellow rain slickers and pants I've seen the fishermen wear. Storm gear."

"You mean like the Gortons' of Gloucester guy. Yellow top and bottom. And boots."

"Yes, him! I've got a picture right here. The big boots could hold the presents."

"We might be desperate, but I don't think that's going to work," Magda said. "What about the reindeer?"

"Leaping dolphins? I don't know. We don't have any reindeer anyway," Mackenzie. "We're in a spot here. If we're going to make this work, we have to believe in it totally. Otherwise nobody else will."

Magda gave a short laugh. "We could just skip Santa this year."

"We have to have Santa. Some version of Santa. We can't disappoint the kids." Her stomach contracted.

"Kids will still have Christmas, you know. We're not their parents."

Some kids might not have any Christmas except for this parade, she thought. "Magda, we can do this," Mackenzie said. "Weave a story. Santa's cousin is taking over for him today because he's busy at the North Pole. Cousin, uh, cousin ..."

"Freddy the Fisherman? Sammy the Sailor?" Magda offered hesitantly.

"Sammy the Sailor! We can do it." Mackenzie said. "I'll tweet it. Do you know anybody with yellow rain gear that might fit Billy Seymour?"

An emergency text to the members of the Village Marketing Group identified the problem. While she was waiting for a response, she drafted special announcements for social media. "Santa's cousin Sammy the Sailor will be at the Sea Stars Festival in Stella Mare today only!"

It was lame but it was better than nothing. Maybe.

When the costume was secured, she'd post the announcements. Then Dorie called. "My dad's got some of that yellow rain gear in the shed. I'll pick it up on the way to the parade ground. It should fit Billy okay. My dad's lost some weight since his fishing days."

"Thank you so much! See you at the campground."

Mackenzie headed toward the east end of the village feeling like she'd dodged a bullet. She pulled into the campground behind a pickup decorated with a pine garland and a big tree with a star on top, wreath hanging from the liftgate and lights jaunty around the cab. Christmas music blared from somewhere. Kids in

Sea Cadets uniforms waved floats into line. She leaned out her window to talk to the pudgy kid on duty.

"Hi. Thanks for helping out today."

The cherub in the uniform grinned. "It's fun. Are you in the parade or just parking?"

"Just parking, please, and I'll need to get out before the parade starts. Where should I go?"

After settling the Corolla near the exit, Mackenzie leashed Murphy and walked briskly back to the action. A bearded man with a clipboard and bullhorn was talking to a man in a firefighter uniform. She waited until they were finished, then approached.

"Kevin?"

"You must be Mackenzie." Kevin stuck out his hand. "Nice to meet you for real."

"Yes it is," she agreed, shaking vigorously. "How's it going here?"

"Good, good," he said. "The floats are checking in. Almost all of them are here already."

"I came by to see how things are going, make sure we're on track," Mackenzie said, "and troubleshoot Santa."

"Santa?"

"Yeah, we've had a costume malfunction already."

He smiled. "Those happen. You learn to do problem-solving on the fly. The big picture for the parade is good. Now all we have to do it get ourselves in line, walk from here to there, and enjoy every step."

Mackenzie couldn't help but smile. "That's a great attitude. It's a parade. It's a festival."

"It's Christmas!" he said with a cheer. "Your Santa wagon is down there, end of the line." He pointed. "The Frankels did a nice job of decorating."

"Thanks," She flashed him a quick smile and started down the long line up of floats. It was a good thing Santa was last in line. That gave her a little more time to pitch the story of Santa's cousin Sammy the Sailor. She hoped the kids would buy it.

She was halfway down the line of floats when she heard Kevin calling her. Turning, she saw him at the head of the line with two older men. Her Santa – now Sammy – had arrived.

"I tole you she was a cute lil' one," Billy slurred. The other man was Russ Johnson who'd originally told her where to find Billy. Billy was leaning heavily on Russ.

"Hi, Billy. Hi, Russ." She didn't say more. Russ planted his feet more firmly and looked sideways at Mackenzie.

"So. Seems like we might have a little situation here," Russ said quietly. "Sorry about this, Mackenzie."

Silence reigned as Mackenzie, Russ, and Kevin looked at Billy. Wobbly despite Russ's firm grip, their would-be Santa gazed at the festive scene. "Looks like Chris'mas here." He stepped away from Russ to fish a silver flask from his back pocket. "Merry Chris'mas. We jus' need a little snow." He gazed into the distance.

"Oh, Russ." Mackenzie groaned. "Oh, no."

"I know," Russ said. "He wanted to come down here. I figured it was better for me to bring him than him try to drive."

Mackenzie sighed as she approached Billy. "Hey, Billy. How are you?"

"What?" Billy squinted as he turned to her voice. "Hey, lil' girl. Yeah, I'm good, I'm good." He took another swig from the flask. "Almos' Chris'mas, ain't it?"

"Yes, it is," she agreed. "A few more days. How do you feel, Billy?"

"Me? M'okay," he said, gazing away from her. "Maybe a little tired."

She turned a questioning gaze on Russ.

"I think he should go home," Russ said. "He's not at his best."

"Yeah. I can see that." Her heart had dropped at Billy's first word. His bleary eyes confirmed the worst, but she was unwilling to concede defeat. "He's only got to sit in the wagon. He doesn't have to do anything. Or say anything."

"You don't want a sloshed Santa." Kevin shook his head.

At that moment, Billy lurched toward Kevin, slung his arm around the other man's shoulders and leaned into him. "Hey, Kev, how's that woman of yours? She's some fine, ain't she?"

Kevin leaned under the man's weight, and Russ stepped in to help keep Billy upright. Mackenzie could imagine the headline in tomorrow's news: Sloshed Santa Makes Waves at Sea Star Festival. She sighed from the bottom of her feet.

Kevin looked at Mackenzie. "I'd recommend letting Russ take him home. The Frankels wouldn't put up with this anyway."

"I'm sure you're right." She also couldn't imagine trying to explain to Billy how Santa had become Sammy the Sailor. "Billy, thank you for coming. I hope you get some rest," she said. Her chest heavy, she turned to Russ to add, "Thanks for bringing him and thanks for taking him home."

Russ took Billy's arm again. "Let's go, Bill. Time to go home, I think."

Mackenzie's throat tightened. She'd seen Russ take her father's arm exactly the same way. Eric, too, had struggled with alcohol. "Russ, how do you always get this job, anyway?"

"Just lucky, I guess," Russ said with a rueful smile. "But I've been in those shoes. And I'm grateful to be sober. To be able to help out."

"Yeah," she said. "Well, Billy's lucky to have you. Dad was, too."

Russ shrugged off her thanks and tugged Billy's arm. "Come on, Billy. Let's take a walk over here." As Russ piloted him away, he spoke to Mackenzie. "Sorry about this."

"It's hardly your fault. He's not well," she said. "Thanks for taking care of him."

As she watched the pair walk away, her shoulders slumped and eyes smarted. This was too much.

"Can we have a Christmas parade without Santa?" she asked Kevin.

"Well, you're not calling it a Christmas parade, are you?" Kevin said practically.

"The advertising said Santa. We already had a costume malfunction that required a new character, but now we don't even have a character."

Kevin snickered. "He's a character all right. But not for our purposes."

"Right," she said, pulling herself upright. "Okay. You're busy here. I'll go explain to the Frankels, but if you get a brainstorm, please text me."

"Not likely," Kevin said and turned to the cluster of teens waiting for his attention. She walked back down the line of floats. It would be okay. It would have to be okay. Maybe Santa's cousin Sammy had to help in the workshop, so neither of them were available for the parade. No, this wasn't working. The story got worse and worse. Who could she get into that wagon?

The Frankels were a multigenerational German-Canadian family from Sussex, whose vegetables graced Market Square all season. They'd dressed for the occasion in old-timey farm clothing covered, of course, with coats, but they'd also decorated the wagon and their draft horses' harness with bells and pine garland. Everything wasn't terrible, she thought. This wagon was lovely.

Charmed, Mackenzie patted a bay on the nose while Murphy wagged his greeting. Together, they walked around the wagon to find Old Mr. Frankel.

"This is beautiful," she said. "You went all out."

Young Mrs. Frankel jumped down beside the wagon. "Well, we're carrying Santa. We recognize the honour. Besides, my daughter is with us, helping my dad. Kids take Santa seriously." She gestured toward a round-faced child of eight who was holding something for Mr. Frankel.

"I need to talk to you about that," she said, glancing toward the child. "Can we talk over here?" The three adults stepped out of the child's earshot.

She explained quickly Santa wasn't coming. "I'm kind of out of ideas now. But if you'll anchor the parade anyway," Mackenzie said, "I'll manage expectations about Santa."

"Maybe you'll find somebody." Old Mr. Frankel was optimistic. "The wagon looks nice anyway. Got that tree on it, and my granddaughter is a pretty girl."

"Do you think she could toss the candy canes?"

"She and I can," her mother said. "Dad does the driving. I was just going to be sitting there in my mobcap and muslin. Don't worry. We can do this."

"Thanks," Mackenzie said. "See you at the Square."

Still full of doubt, she walked back toward the front of the parade, looking at her phone. A text from Declan popped up.

How's it going? Not much excitement here at school.

She called him. "Hey."

"Hey. How are things?" The sound of his voice plucked at the fragile thread of her emotional control. Nearly undone, she swallowed hard. "It's pretty awful. Disastrous, I'd say."

"What happened? Are you hurt?"

"Me? No, I'm fine." Why would he worry about her? "I'm at the parade line-up. Things were bad but now they're worse. The Santa suit was full of pee and Santa full of vodka. No Santa for the parade. The kids are going to be so disappointed." She stifled a sob.

"Oh, Mackenzie." Was he chuckling? She felt a spurt of anger.

"Don't you dare laugh. This is serious."

"No, I'm not laughing. I get it. You were expecting Santa and it's not happening."

"Right."

"But you know, the kids will survive. Everything doesn't have to be perfect."

"How can you have a Christmas parade without Santa, though? It's just not right."

He sighed. "How are you doing?"

"Right now, things stink. I'm still trying to figure it out."

"Can I help?"

She wanted him to come be with her. That would make everything feel better, but she knew he was busy. "That's sweet and I appreciate the offer. But you've got your stuff to do. It'll be okay. I'll be okay. There's a lot that's going well, too."

"I'll see you at school later on, then," he said. "Love you."

"Love you, too." She clicked off and gazed at her phone, walking down the line of floats, Murphy by her side.

"Mackenzie! Mackenzie, you're going to trip. Look up!"

"Hi, Dorie," she said, walking toward the Dog Sanctuary van and mustering a smile. "The van looks great."

Dorie's white poodle danced at her feet, as if to show off his fancy Christmas collar and the flashing lights he wore. He and Murphy touched noses.

"Dorie, could Murphy do the parade with you? He's been with me all day, but I think he might need to sit the parade out."

"Sure," Dorie said. "He and Frou-Frou can look cute together in the van. By the way, I've got the storm gear right here," Dorie said, opening the rear doors.

"I hate to tell you, but we don't have anybody to wear it. Santa was a little under the weather."

"Billy was drunk again?"

"You expected that? Nobody warned me," she said. "I never even considered..."

"Sorry," Dorie said. "He's unreliable. I should have told you."

Don't count on anybody, Mackenzie heard her mother saying. You can only count on yourself. "I should have guessed. But now I have no Santa, and not even Sammy the Sailor."

"Sammy the Sailor was a stretch anyway," Dorie said.

"It was a reach born of desperation. Probably nobody would buy it anyway. Kids won't believe Santa's cousin Sammy is filling in." Her heart dropped again. "I just posted all those messages about him, too."

Dorie looked concerned. "Can I offer Chad? He's not exactly outgoing, but maybe he could do it."

"Do what?" Chad asked, coming around the back of the van.

Dorie lifted her chin. "I might have just volunteered you to be Sammy the Sailor in place of Santa. What do you think?"

His expression said more than his words, which were mild. "I'm already working the parade, Dorie."

"I can handle the van and the dogs," she said. "Mackenzie needs a Santa-type guy."

"I'm doing the video," he reminded her. "Drone and handheld."

"Don't worry, Chad," Mackenzie said. "We'll figure something out. Thanks, both of you. I'll take the storm suit anyway, in case we find somebody."

Dorie piled the heavy gear into her arms and then invited the dogs into the van. Mackenzie headed back toward the Frankel's wagon, but before she got there, the parade was already moving. She tossed the gear in the back of the wagon with a word of explanation to Young Mrs. Frankel and took off at a run for her Corolla. She needed to be downtown.

She parked a couple of blocks off Water Street, which was already blocked off to traffic, then sprinted toward Market Square. Daylight dimmed even at four fifteen amd the streetlights were coming on. Makenzie stopped across the street from Market Square to gaze toward the water. The front window of Dakin's Hardware was full of twinkly lights, and a soft glow came from the Fishburn Gallery. Market Square itself was bursting with food stalls, food trucks, and wonderful aromas. People filled the street, wandering, laughing, and talking. Music spilled from one of the shops. Despite her worry, Mackenzie felt her heart lift as she took in the festive atmosphere. Santa or not, it was almost Christmas.

She couldn't appreciate for long, though, because the distant sounds of the pipe and drum band reminded her she still needed someone to pull the giveaway winner and praise Josiah for his civic generosity. The speech still needed edits. She scrambled for her notepad.

What if Magda didn't show up? As the sounds from the parade drew closer, the thought of making the speech herself made her feel ill. I'd rather die, she thought, than get up in front of this crowd, especially after disappointing them with no Santa.

"Mackenzie!" Charlie Dakin waved from the door of the hardware store. "Come on over!" She headed across the crowded street.

"Good job," Charlie boomed. "Look at all these folks. People having a good time."

"Great," she said. "It looks like it's going okay."

"Not just okay," he insisted. "It's going great. Now, when are we going to get our prize for the best decorated window?"

Suddenly breathless, Mackenzie held up one finger. "We'll be letting you know," she said, and walked off into the crowd. One more dropped ball.

Her phone buzzed. Magda. *On my way with the entries. Do you have a container?*

I'm going to die from details, she thought. *I'll have one.* She went back to the hardware store.

By the time Magda appeared in the square, arms full of giveaway entries, Mackenzie held a beribboned red feed bucket courtesy of Dakin's Hardware.

"Excellent," Magda approved. "Now we just need somebody to pull the winner."

"And decide who won the window decorating contest," Mackenzie added somberly.

Magda stared at her. "We forgot that, too, didn't we?"

"I did," she said miserably.

"Well, it's not Christmas until Wednesday, so we'll announce the winner on Christmas Eve," Magda said. "That'll give the executive committee time to decide."

"Thank you," Mackenzie said with relief. "Billy couldn't do Santa or Sammy the Sailor," she added.

"Drunk, eh?"

Mackenzie shook her head. "Why didn't anybody tell me? It seems like everybody knew it except for me."

"He's a perfect Santa," Magda said, "except he can be unreliable. He can't help it."

Their phones buzzed in unison. "Uh, oh," Mackenzie said. "What now?"

"No uh oh about it," Magda said, grinning. "Look at what Chad's posting. It's a livestream."

The livestream link showed drone footage of the parade moving down Water Street with festive lights, music, and the firetruck full of uniformed firefighters waving at children. "Live from Stella Mare," Magda said with a satisfied smile. "This is great."

Mackenzie took a screen shot and posted it with a note: "It's not too late! You can still get here in time for the high school play and the Sea Stars Ball!"

She leaned to peer down Water Street. The leading police car was visible. The parade was coming. "This is it," she said to Magda. "Did I tell you that I am never doing this again?"

Magda laughed. "It's going great. Besides, next year we'll be experts. Ooops, I missed the chocolate shop." Magda took the giveaway bucket across the street to collect the last of the entries.

Mackenzie gazed at the crowd watching and waiting for the parade. A man stood with three bundled-up children, holding the littlest one in his arms.

"Santa's coming, right, Daddy?" The tall girl said. "We're going to see Santa."

"Santa!" the toddler in his arms shouted. "Santa."

Mackenzie's stomach plummeted again. All the tweets in the world wouldn't prepare every child for this ultimate disappointment.

The crowd cheered as the police cruiser eased past Market Square toward the hill leading to the high school. Cheers rang out for each of the floats. The firetruck got gasps of awe from the kids. When firefighters in uniform walking alongside handed out candy canes, enthusiasm grew.

Mackenzie was counting floats. The wagon was last, and its arrival meant time for the speech, the draw for the giveaway basket and, worst, facing the disappointment about a missing Santa.

Oh, her edits! The speech needed to include Josiah and the food drive. Should Magda apologize for Santa's absence? She scribbled on her tablet in the dim light under the streetlamp.

The wave of sound intensified as the parade neared the end. The pipe and drum band marched by in kilts, shivering but loud. The high school climate change float was next, the last float before the Frankel's wagon. Cheers and shouts accompanied the teens and their massive papier-mâché Earth. Loud recorded music played from their float. She heard them go by as she was finishing her changes.

She looked up to see the draft horses tossing their manes, bells jangling from the harness. Old Mr. Frankel drove the wagon, looking like something out of the seventeenth century. The kids near her were squealing. "Santa! Santa!"

Heaving a sigh, she glanced over to see their disappointed faces, but all three kids were glowing. She followed their gaze upward to the back of the hay wagon, past the lighted fir tree, past Young Mrs. Frankel and her daughter tossing candy canes to see somebody else. Another person sat in the wagon, a big person with a red suit and a long white beard. Waving his gloved hands at the crowd.

She gasped. There was Santa, firmly in place on a bale of straw. How could it be? Shaking her head and smiling as if her face would crack, her tears were close. Maybe Christmas miracles did happen. Just never to her. Until now.

"Santa!" She waved and called out like the children. Santa caught her eye, but before she could process what she saw, the wagon was past her. The other floats paused heading up the hill, but Old Mr. Frankel directed the horses into the square and turned them around, Santa still waving from the back. The crowd surged toward the wagon, Mackenzie out in front.

"Santa?" she said tentatively.

"Ho, ho, ho!" boomed Declan.

She started laughing and crying at the same time. "I am so glad to see you, Santa," she said.

"Ho, ho, ho, little lady," he said in the same big booming voice, winking. Kids were all around the wagon, waving and shouting. Somebody bumped her left elbow, and she looked around to see Magda.

Surprise and delight played across her friend's face. "Look at that," she said. "Santa showed up. Who is it?"

"It's Santa," Mackenzie said. "Magda, your timing is impeccable. It's time for the draw and the speech. I've made some last minute edits."

"More edits?" Magda said. "Now?"

"Had to happen. We're going with the flow, right?"

"Not my best thing," Magda acknowledged. "But okay. Let's have it."

"I've got it right here," Mackenzie said. "Let Santa pick the winner and you announce it. And here's the amended speech. Okay?"

Magda sighed. "Sure. Why not?"

"Thanks!" Mackenzie gave her a quick hug and handed over her tablet.

Magda looked up at the wagon, dubious. "Do I have to climb up there?"

"I will help you." Old Mr. Frankel, courtly, got down from the driver's seat to hand her up. She clambered into the back of the wagon and Mackenzie handed up the red feed bucket.

Chad appeared at Mackenzie's right hand, holding the clip-on microphone. "Tell her to use this."

"How did you know we needed this?" Mackenzie asked as she and Mr. Frankel passed the wireless mic to Magda. "Never mind. You can explain later."

Chad shrugged and smiled, and Magda tapped the mic. It was live.

"Now or never," Mackenzie said. "You got this."

She stepped back to watch and listen. People crowded Market Square, spilling down from Water Street. The food trucks were busy; the place smelled wonderful. Excited kids bounced, pulling on their parents and asking to be lifted up. Glancing around, she saw Dorie's sister Evie standing against the wall by the gallery, Cassandra beside her. She lifted her hand, and Cassandra returned the wave.

This was it, the culmination of the Sea Stars Festival. It was time to thank people, to wrap up, send people off to watch the play and go to the Ball, but the downtown events – her parts – were just about over. She couldn't shed her tension, though. Magda still had that speech to read, and there was the draw, and the window contest, and all those things. It wasn't over, exactly, but she really had nothing else to do. Maybe it was time to try to enjoy it.

She lifted her chin toward the wagon. Dear, dear Declan. She swiped at her eyes.

As her vision cleared, she saw flakes in the air. Snow flurries, the light, fluffy kind. Talk about a Hallmark moment. White flakes dusted Santa's shoulders.

A police constable urged the crowd away from the wagon as Magda called for attention. "Happy Sea Stars Festival! Welcome to our village, and thank you for celebrating with us! Attention, please."

The crowd gradually quieted. From Mackenzie's vantage point at the side of the square, she saw Josiah push to the front of the crowd, stepping in front of a cluster of little boys. Scouring the group behind him, she finally located Estelle, arms folded, leaning against a brick wall, not far from Mackenzie. She wondered briefly how well Estelle would handle a surprise, but her attention returned to Magda immediately.

"Welcome and thank you all for coming to the first-ever Stella Mare Sea Stars Festival. We hope you enjoy your visit. We'd like to see you return over and over to our little Star of the Sea, right here in New Brunswick.

"An event like this can only happen because people come together for good. I have the pleasure of thanking those who helped create today's festival. The Sea Stars Festival was sponsored by the Village Marketing Group and supported by the Village board of selectmen and the downtown business community. Thank you also for the support of the entire village for that wonderful parade."

Magda paused and the crowd politely clapped and cheered. "Thanks also to Saint James Church, the Stella Mare Campground, and all our volunteers. In just about five minutes, Santa will draw the name of the winner of our giveaway basket. Charlie, can you show us that prize basket? What's in there?"

It was more than a basket. It was a whole wagon load, a red wagon, pulled by Charlie Dakin up alongside the Frankels' wagon. Charlie had a big voice, easily heard by Mackenzie despite having no microphone. "Yessir, Magda, we got quite a wagonful. You can see we got a whole lotta stuff for some lucky winner. This here wagon load."

"Tell us what's in the wagon, Charlie," Magda prompted.

"Well, in here we got some chocolate from McGuire's, a pottery mug Mrs. Innskeep made, a painting by Evie Madison, a box of cinnamon rolls from the Sunshine Diner, and look at this! A bright red hot chocolate maker."

He held it up as if he'd never seen it. Mackenzie snickered to herself. *Charlie could have made that speech. I'll put him on the list for next year.*

He continued. "And there's a watering can in there, and I think some gift certificates for high tea at the hotel, and dinner at the Shore House. Pretty good basket."

"Okay, Santa," Magda said, holding up the red feed bucket. "I've shaken and shuffled all the entries. Pick a good one!"

Santa, standing, removed his glove and swished his hand in the bucket. He caught Mackenzie's eye as he pulled. She couldn't tell for sure under the beard, but she thought he wore a big smile. He handed the card to Magda.

She read it, coughed, and looked at it again. "Well, our giveaway winner is Mr. Billy Seymour," she read loudly, looking directly at Mackenzie with a grin. "Congratulations to our friend, Billy Seymour!"

The crowd cheered, and Mackenzie giggled, then giggles gave way to big belly laughs that made her double over. Gales of laughter released weeks of tension, but she had to compose herself. Things weren't over yet. By an act of will, she stifled her laughter and wiped at her eyes. There was more to come.

Magda, composed, went on. "The Village Marketing group would like to thank Mr. Josiah Steeves for his support of the food drive. Josiah, do you want to say something?"

Oh, no, Mackenzie thought, suddenly completely serious. That wasn't in the playbook.

Josiah demurred for half a second, but soon climbed the wheel of the wagon to take the mic from Magda.

"Thank you, there, and I wanted to remind everyone it's the season for believin' and I 'preciate all the fine folks shopping at the Save Mart and putting food in the basket. Not everybody has the means to help, but we can all do what we can. There's folks will have a happy Christmas because of you. I believe we have to help each other and buying groceries at the Save Mart helps. Thank you for doing your part."

That was the most peculiar, convoluted, self-serving speech she'd ever heard, but who was she to judge? Besides, Magda had said the point was to give Josiah a chance to feel good about what he was doing. Maybe he was doing his best.

Magda retrieved the mic and went on. "Thank you, Josiah. Let's show Josiah our thanks, everybody!" She led the way with applause, while Josiah, smug, waved at the crowd.

Magda waited for the applause to die down and continued. "We have something a little different to talk about now," she said. "The Saint James Church ladies auxiliary are assembling Christmas baskets from the food drive that Josiah sponsored and food collected at the church. Thank you for all you do.

"We wanted to make a special mention of our support for the Sea Widows and Orphans Fund. This worthy organization was founded in 1970 by our own Estelle Steeves. Is Estelle here?" Magda looked around. "Estelle, if you're here, give us a wave."

Gazing across the square, Mackenzie willed Estelle to wave. *Come on, come on.* Estelle tucked her chin down into her collar.

"Maybe she's not here," Magda improvised. "Anyway, we all know fishing is a hard life, and the sea claims lives. We've probably all lost someone. When the lost one leaves behind a family, the suffering continues. The Sea Widows fund helps support these families. Thank you to Estelle for your efforts through the years and thank you, everyone, for your support!" Over applause, Magda added, "When you see Estelle over at the Save Mart, make sure to thank her for her volunteer work."

There was more applause.

"The festivities go on! Don't forget the world premiere of *Diving Deep* by playwright Declan Kelly in the high school auditorium. After the play, join the Sea Stars Ball in the high school gym. Or you can stay downtown, enjoy the food and the fun. Shops are open until nine tonight. Happy festival! Thanks for coming, everyone!"

The crowd began to disperse, and Mackenzie looked back to where she'd last seen Estelle. She was almost afraid to look for the woman. Before she could dissect her own feelings, Estelle appeared at her shoulder.

"You did read that paper," she said.

"It wasn't easy to read, but then I found the website. You started that whole thing. A movement. A registered charity."

Estelle shrugged. "You give what you can. I understood widows. Single mothers. Like yours."

"And Declan's."

Estelle's eyes widened, then she gave a brief nod. "Yes. Your man. I forgot he was one of ours. There are more than we know."

"Why aren't you working with them now?" Mackenzie asked. "Just busy?"

Estelle gave a one-shouldered shrug. "I had my boys. The store. Josiah."

Mackenzie thought about Josiah and his sour look when she asked for donations. "I can see how that might interfere. I hope the village will continue to support the group, though."

Estelle gave a tight nod. "I would have let the food drive go on today, if I knew you were donating to Sea Widows," Estelle said. "I might have been a bit short."

"Maybe next year, the whole food drive can go there. Now that we know about it, I can't think of a better charity for Stella Mare to support."

Estelle nodded again, unsmiling. Turning, she walked into the dusk, snowflakes dusting the shoulders of her dark coat.

"Merry Christmas, Estelle," Mackenzie called out.

The older woman turned all the way back. A smile touched her lips. "Yeah. Merry Christmas." Mackenzie watched as she disappeared into the crowd.

The Frankels' wagon finally pulled out of the square to follow the rest of the floats up the hill, all moving faster now the parade was over. Mackenzie missed catching up with Santa. Before she'd even made it across Market Square, Magda grabbed her elbow.

"Hey."

"Hey." They looked at each other, and then Magda grabbed Mackenzie in a hug. "Good work, partner."

"Thanks. You did a great job on the speech," Mackenzie said, hugging back.

"I can say the same. It's easy if you have a good speechwriter. I think it went great. Good job. Well done. All over." She patted Mackenzie's back and released her.

"Not really all over," Mackenzie objected. "The play, the ball...clean-up."

"You're not responsible for any of those things. Your job is done."

Mackenzie let those words settle in. "Really? My job is done. I'm not responsible. That feels good."

"We did great! You made a wonderful festival happen, and you should be proud. Good job!"

"Well, there were some issues," she said tightly.

Magda frowned. "Now is the time to look at what went well. We can work from lessons learned next time."

Mackenzie's shoulders dropped down from her ears. "Yes. We can look at the issues later."

"Right. For now, good work!" Magda cheered.

"Thank you. We did it, didn't we?"

"We sure did."

Cassandra bounced up behind Magda. "Hey. Nice job!"

"Thank you. How were things at the Sunshine?" Mackenzie asked.

"Busy. We were slammed, just like I hoped. But the parade was the most fun. How did you keep Santa a secret? I thought it was going to be Billy Seymour."

Mackenzie grinned at her and Magda. "So did we. But I'm learning to be flexible. To trust that things might work out."

Magda looked puzzled. "Who was it? How did we even have a Santa in a Santa suit?"

"It was Declan, but I have no idea how he pulled it off."

"I barely recognized him," Cassandra said, "and I've known him my whole life."

"Well, he saved the day for the kids, anyway," Magda said.

"For me, too," Mackenzie added, heartfelt.

"That's a good boyfriend. Where are you headed now?"

"It's closing night at the play," she said. "Can't miss it. Cassandra and I are going together. Will we see you at the ball?"

Magda nodded. "You bet, but first Jesse and I are having dinner and a well-earned glass of wine. Well, mine will be well-earned. I'll see you both later tonight." She left.

Fatigue flowed into Mackenzie's limbs. "I think it went okay."

"It was great. Not okay. Give yourself some credit," Cassandra insisted. "I bet you haven't eaten all day, have you?"

"Food! What a great idea. We've got a little while before the play."

The evening was getting colder, but the red plush, belly padding and scratchy beard meant Declan was plenty warm, maybe too warm. His heart felt warm, too, thinking about Mackenzie's face when she saw Santa on the wagon and, again, when she recognized him in this fuzzy suit. As the wagon lumbered up and over the hill, following the last of the floats, he struggled to stay in character for the few kids who still lined the street. Surreptitiously peeking at his watch, he felt a growing alarm. The clop-clop of the draft horses' feet on pavement was soothing, but he still needed to get to school.

He turned to Young Mrs. Frankel, also known as Beatrice, a former classmate of his. "I've got to get going," he said. "Thanks for everything."

"See you, Dec," she said. "You're a pretty good Santa."

Her daughter grinned at him. "Yeah, not bad. Will you be my teacher when I get to high school?"

"Probably," he said. "You've got a few years yet."

He was relieved he wasn't ruining her childhood dreams of Santa by running off. He leaned up to thank Old Mr. Frankel and jumped out of the slowly moving wagon.

It wasn't far to walk, but it was uphill and he was wearing a Santa suit. Still aware of children, he started off at a jog, but the jostling made his belly shift around so part of it fell down his pants. This was not working. Finally, he ducked into a space between two houses and shucked the red fleece. He emerged as himself, with a big pile of costuming in his arms. At least this way he could make better progress up the hill. When he finally got to the high school, he'd worked up a big sweat.

He dropped the suit off in the storage closet that held years of drama club costumes. Old dinosaur heads, the Crown Jewels of some imaginary monarchy, and assorted dresses, suits, hats, and footwear had been dumped everywhere, evidence of his desperate search for a Santa costume earlier in the day. He'd sort it all out later. Right now, the show was about to go on.

Mackenzie let Cassandra lead the way into the auditorium, choosing seats near the middle. It was a great place to watch the audience assemble. She sank into her chair, comfortably warm, fed, and finally beginning to relax after her long day outdoors. She waved to Dorie and Chad over to her left, and Cassandra pointed out Leonard Fishburne, the owner of the art gallery.

"Is that Evie with him?"

Cassandra looked again. "Yes, it's Evie and her boyfriend, Stephen. Stephen lives upstairs over the gallery, at least for now." She turned to Mackenzie. "You ought to meet him. He's an American, too."

Mackenzie laughed. "It's a big country. There're a lot of us."

"Yes, and a lot of you guys here in the Maritimes, too."

"Well, that's probably because of shared history."

"And shared ancestry. My grandparents were back-to-the-landers down toward Sussex. They came from Connecticut in the 1960s."

"Really?" Mackenzie, intrigued, pulled her attention away from Evie, Stephen, and Leonard, who were chatting together like a family. "You're part American?"

Cassandra shook her head. "No, but my grandparents were. Kind of secretive about it, too. Maybe they were avoiding Vietnam."

"Maybe," Mackenzie said hesitantly. "Then there was my father, a Canadian, who crossed the border the other way so he could join the army. Times were different then."

"Well, Stephen isn't a back-to-the-lander. He's like an art anthropologist for his university. He's from North Carolina."

"That's what Evie said." Mackenzie gazed back toward the trio across the way. "I bet winter's cold for him."

Snickering, Cassandra said, "It's cold for everybody, but he arrived last March, so he's had a good dose."

"Last year was my first winter," Mackenzie said. "I was cold all the time. At least now I'm better prepared. Oh, it's starting."

The lights dipped, the announcements were made and, as the curtain drew back, Mackenzie was immediately drawn into the play. Cassandra's gasps and giggles as the events unfolded on stage made it like seeing the show for the first time again. This performance was golden. It seemed all the kinks were gone, the kids were in flow, and the play lifted her out of her fatigue and into the story.

When the final curtain fell, Mackenzie handed tissues to her sniffling companion as waves of applause washed over the auditorium from the standing crowd. Standing and cheering, Mackenzie felt right at home, part of a whole community.

The man directly in front of Cassandra was vociferous, clapping and cheering. He turned around to them, saying, "Did you see that? That's my boy!"

Mackenzie nodded. "It was wonderful." He didn't respond, just telling anyone around him, "That's my boy, that one. Great job!"

"That's one supportive dad," Cassandra whispered to Mackenzie. Lucky kid who had a dad like that, she thought. I wonder...She leaned forward to tug on the man's sleeve.

"Which one is your boy?"

He smiled even wider and pointed. "The boy who saved the village. Chuck. My boy Charles, Junior. Chuck."

Oh, Chuck, Mackenzie thought. Untucked Chuck? Well, well, well.

"He was wonderful," she said truthfully to the proud father.

The ovation continued through the entire curtain call, only subsiding when Patrice, still swathed in tulle as the Queen of the Bay, called for quiet. Two girls ran offstage, re-emerging with huge bouquets. Patrice called Mrs. MacRae to come up, and then Mr. Kelly. Speeches of gratitude were brief, but there were many onstage hugs. The audience added their unreserved enthusiasm. Mackenzie watched about six teenage girls clutch Declan, who held his flowers in the other hand, looking dazed. She giggled. "Declan looks so uncomfortable."

Cassandra nudged her. "Stop it. Don't you remember having a crush on your handsome high school teacher?"

"Maybe," Mackenzie said. "I would have been too shy to hug him."

The house lights came up and the audience began to gather belongings, trickling out of their seats, stopping in clusters for conversation, hugs, and greetings. It made for slow going when Mackenzie followed Cassandra toward the aisle. When she glanced at the stage, though, she stopped in her tracks. Aurora was hugging Declan, clinging to his neck, really, while his hands were decidedly at his sides. She nudged Cassandra.

"Look at that."

"Eeewww," her friend said. "She was weird even when I was a student. That's gross."

"Well, it'll give the kids something to talk about," she said lightly, but it was disturbing.

"Maybe the parents, too. That's really not okay. Let's go to the stage door," Cassandra urged.

"Sure. That'll be fun," Mackenzie said. "The play was great, wasn't it? The kids should be so proud."

"Being here reminds me of my high school set designing days. I can show you the mural that Evie Madison did back in the day. I also want to congratulate the playwright."

Mackenzie wrestled her attention away from the stage and followed.

Backstage had cleared out before Declan checked himself for his belongings: coat, phone, keys to the truck. He wondered if he had to take that big bunch of flowers home, but then decided Mackenzie might like them. Tucking them under his arm, he looked around backstage, picked up a few papers, and headed for the stage door.

Clusters of actors and parents and friends hung just inside the door, and when he went through into the corridor, there were more people. He scanned the crowd.

"There he is! Mr. Playwright!" Cassandra called to him from behind a small group. She was dressed all in black as usual.

He walked around toward her, arms out for a big hug. He hugged her, but his eyes were on Mackenzie just behind, looking exhausted and happy. When Cassandra released him, he held his arms out and Mackenzie sank into them. He rested his face on her hair, and held on tightly, eyes closed.

"Okay, you guys," Cassandra said. "Come on now. You've got to let people congratulate you. What a great day! What a great play."

With regret, he opened his eyes to see Cassandra holding up her phone.

"Are you taking our picture?" he demanded. Mackenzie turned to look.

"Of course I am," Cassandra said. "Want to see?" She handed over the phone, and he and Mackenzie peered together.

"It's grey, Cass," Mackenzie objected. "We're both grey."

"That's art," Cassandra declared. "It's an artistic decision to filter you in the colour and atmosphere you project."

"Wait a minute," Declan said. "Who are you calling boring?"

"Who said boring? Not boring. Fatigued."

Mackenzie pulled the phone toward her. "Well, you might be onto something. You could title that picture 'Exhaustion' and win a prize." She smiled at Declan. "Yes, I'm tired, but guess what! We made it."

His face felt like it might split open, he was smiling so hard. "We did. We sure did."

"The play was great, Declan. I didn't know you wrote like that," Cassandra said. "I thought you did historical stuff, not fantasy."

He shrugged. "I try out different things. I'm glad you liked it. The kids did great."

"They did," Mackenzie agreed. "Fixed every issue and made it even better."

He nodded. "Thinking about what you want rather than getting stuck on what could go wrong...that is a good model. Works for me."

Cassandra's phone made a noise. "Oh, my buddy's here for the ball," she said. "You two are coming, right?"

"In a little while," Declan said.

"Okay, see you there." She flipped a hand and headed through the thinning crowd. People were filing out of the auditorium wing. The ball was on the other side of the school, music already faintly audible.

He took Mackenzie's hand. "So, Cinderella, do you want to go to the Ball?"

She gazed up at him. "How did you do it?"

"Do what? Oh, you mean Santa." He scoffed. "Dumb luck, really. I dug around in the costume closet and there was Santa. Pat helped me get the stuffing right and dropped me off at the campground. That's all that happened."

"You saved the day. Thinking about all the kids not having Santa, well, that just about killed me, that disappointment."

Her face reflected all those tiny, borrowed Christmases of her childhood, the light of hope shrinking year to year. He tucked a finger under her chin. "You looked pretty happy to see Santa yourself."

She lit up again as she chuckled. "You have no idea. It was like everything I'd ever wanted had just worked out."

"Everything?"

"Well, everything a kid dreams about. You know how when you're a kid, you learn not to want too much because you get disappointed? I was feeling all the disappointment of all those kids –"

"That you were imagining," he interjected.

"Yes, but still feeling it. I know the kids standing beside me would have been devastated if there was no Santa."

"And then there was Santa."

She brightened again. "There was Santa, making the child in me so happy. When Santa turned out to be you, well, that was the cherry on top. That made all of me very happy. You can't imagine what that was like."

"Maybe I can," he said. Looking at the light in her eyes now, he remembered her darkness when they'd first met. Her hope for a family had been nearly extinguished, and finding her father didn't relight it the way either of them expected. Over time, he'd seen her come back to life as she found her people, and him. He wondered if she feared it could disappear any moment.

She needed to know he wasn't going anywhere. He tightened his grasp on her hand. "So, do you want to go to the Ball? With me?"

She leaned into him. "Of course I do. But first I have to give you something."

"What is that?"

"A really good kiss. A Christmas kiss."

He looked around the empty corridor. "Here?"

"Here is as good a place as any." He waited, watching her eyes as she moved closer, then he let himself ease into the softness of her lips, and the increasing pressure of her arms wrapped around him. The hallway receded as he soaked her in. The warmth of her leaning into him, the tender skin of her face, her lips, teeth, tongue, searching, luxuriating. Time must have passed, but it was hard to tell, and when she pulled back, he opened his eyes. Hers were soft, dreamy, and a little smile touched her face. "How was that?"

"That was a really good kiss."

She changed clothes in the girls' washroom near the gym. The institutional green walls and disinfectant aroma reminded her of her own high school. She slipped into her dressy dress and sparkly flats, stuffing her play-watching clothes into her backpack. Her shoulders felt the weight of her long day, but excitement burbled in her belly. The festival was over, the play was over, and now it was, well, it was almost Christmas. Time for fun.

Her mind felt full of the day, though; the kids at the square waiting for Santa, the gut-punch of seeing and hearing Billy at the staging grounds, Estelle's tiny smile as she said, "Merry Christmas." So much stirred around inside her she fumbled her earrings and couldn't find her lipstick.

A bang at the door made her jump. "Mackenzie? You okay?" Declan sounded worried.

"Yes, I'll be right there," she called back, shaking out her hair. "You'll have to do," she said to her reflection in the spotted glass of the mirror. Dropping her shoulders, she pushed open the door.

Declan was looking away, down the hall, fiddling with a cuff link. She let the door swing back behind her as she soaked in the sight. Declan in a jacket and tie. And French cuffs! Who knew he was going to go all out for the ball? She was glad for her blingy footwear.

Before she could speak, he turned to look at her. His jaw fell and eyes went wide, but she wondered if she was wearing the same expression.

A voice came down the hallway before either of them could speak. "Where's that Mr. Kelly? I have a few things to say to him," a man grumbled.

Declan, alert, called back, "I'm right here." He gave Mackenzie a "what the heck?" look. The man walked heavily down the hall, hat in his hands, and Mackenzie suddenly recognized him from the auditorium. She wondered if Declan knew who he was.

"I'm Declan Kelly," Declan said.

The man stopped short. "I want a word with you." His voice was grim. Mackenzie scooted to Declan's side, tucking her fingers inside his hand.

"How can I help you?" Declan asked easily.

The man was big, taller than Declan by half a head, and heavy, with broad shoulders. He no longer felt threatening to Mackenzie, though, despite his growl.

"I know you," he said. "You crewed for Russ Johnson last summer."

Declan nodded. "A couple of weeks. I don't think we met, though."

"Maybe not then. But now we need to have a few words."

"Sure," Declan agreed.

"Mr. Kelly, you did something to my son," he said.

"I did?" Declan leaned back a little and his fingers tightened on Mackenzie's.

The man nodded. "You and that there Pat MacRae. Playacting." He nearly spit out the word. "You made him into an actor."

"Drama club...." Declan started to explain, but then said, "Who is your son?"

The man's face softened. "Charles, Junior. The kid who saved the village."

Declan's face opened into a wide smile. "You're Chuck's dad." He stuck his hand out to shake. "I am so happy to meet you. You've got a great kid there."

The other man hesitated a moment, but then clasped Declan's hand with both of his. "I would never have said this before, but you did a good thing with that boy. I didn't know he had it in him. For sure his old man isn't an actor. Heck, I've hardly even gone to any plays except this one."

"Chuck did a good job with his part," Declan said, "but he did a lot of other things, too, Mr. Thibodeau. He was a vital part of the drama team. He pulled his weight and then some."

Mr. Thibodeau nodded. "The boy's good out on the boat, too. You want to have him beside you. I have to admit, though, if I'da known he was acting, I'd have put my foot down."

"You didn't know?"

"I sure didn't. Chuck and his mom kept me in the dark. My wife said I wouldn't have understood. She mighta been right."

"I'm very glad Chuck got to be in the play." Declan was firm. "He made an important contribution."

"Well, now, thank you kindly. I was surprised to see how he was up on stage. Speaking right out. Saving the village, that was something." He wiped his eyes.

"Chuck really made that part come to life," Mackenzie added.

"You don't know your little boy is grown up until you see him on the stage, saving the world," he said. He sniffed and put his hat on. "Mr. Kelly, you might be a good playwriter, but you're also a good teacher. Chuck tells me you're gonna go to New York and write books and whatnot, but I think you should reconsider. This school needs you. You opened up my eyes. A good thing for me and my boy, too."

New York! Mackenzie could hardly breathe. When had Declan said he wanted to go to New York?

"Thank you." Declan's voice was thick.

"Yup," Chuck's dad acknowledged, then took a step back. "Well, I can see you two are heading to that dance. I won't keep you." He started down the hallway, then looked back over his shoulder. "You clean up pretty good, too."

"Thanks." There was a grin in Declan's voice. Mr. Thibodeau, heavy-footed, tromped away, Mackenzie gazing after him.

She turned to find Declan gazing at her. "You clean up pretty good there," he said solemnly.

"New York?"

"Broadway, of course, as the next step after Stella Mare. It was a joke, but Chuck might have taken me seriously. Why would I go anywhere when I've got the prettiest girl in the world right here?"

She decided to let it go. Tilting her head, she tossed her hair over her shoulder with a flirtatious smile, ala Aurora Smithers. "So, do you want to go dancing?"

"When you look at me like that, I'll do whatever you want," he said.

"Take that, Ms. Smithers," she said.

Sunday

The sun came up at eight as usual on Sunday, but Mackenzie and Declan were still asleep. Murphy nosed one side of the bed and then the other, but Mackenzie managed to ignore his canine hints until he took a mighty leap and landed in between them.

"Whoa, there," Declan said sleepily.

Mackenzie opened her eyes to the dog flopped on their bed, Declan's face close to the golden fur, and his laughing eyes looking her way.

"Guess it's morning," she said, then yawned and stretched. "Oh, cold out there," she noted as her arms chilled immediately.

"I'll do it," Declan said. "You stay here until the house warms up. Come on, Murph, I'll let you out. At least you waited until the sun came up." He climbed out from under the duvet and hurriedly pulled on flannel pants and a sweatshirt. "December is too cold to sleep naked," he said over his shoulder.

She raised her eyebrows. "It's warm as long as you stay tucked in," she said.

"You look so comfortable," he said. "I feel like climbing back in."

Murphy barked a short reminder. "But the dog," Mackenzie said.

Footsteps and toenails clattered down the stairs and Mackenzie turned over, pulling her pillow under her shoulder. She usually got up first, so it was sweet Declan got the stove going before she had to move. Maybe he'd even make coffee, she thought with a jolt of pleasure.

Soon the warm air penetrated the upstairs along with the fragrance of coffee, and she felt suddenly both too warm and lonely under the duvet.

Declan was stirring something in the sunny kitchen. The pellet stove exuded warmth, and the coffee scent made Mackenzie lightheaded. She slid into a chair at the old table.

"Hey," Declan said. "Coffee?"

"You bet," she agreed. He fussed around a bit, then presented her favourite mug, where he'd made a heart in her latte foam.

"I didn't know you could do this," she said, gesturing. "It's beautiful."

"Not too beautiful to drink, I hope," he said seriously.

"Never," she agreed fervently, and took a sip. "Cassandra better watch out," she said. "You make a great barista."

He poured his own, then sat across from her. "So, all that's left now is Christmas," he said.

She tensed immediately. "You mean Christmas dinner."

He shrugged. "Well, all the parts of Christmas. I think we've put it off as long as we could. Let's get our tree today."

Excitement shot through her. "Our very own tree! We don't have anything to put on it."

"We can shop a little in town," he said. "Old folks used to string popcorn and cranberries, too."

She perked up. "Right. I remember my mother talking about that. Charlie has decorations at the hardware store, too."

By noon, they were ready for a trip to town. "It's Mackenzie and Declan's Big Christmas Adventure!" Declan declared. Murphy whined. "Oh, right. Mackenzie, Declan, and Murphy's adventure."

The dog jumped into the pickup, settling down behind the seats. Declan's playlist filled the truck cab with Christmas music as they headed down the shore road into town. He hummed along as he drove, singing out when he knew the words, and looking sideways at Mackenzie.

She smiled back. "I didn't learn many of these songs."

"I did," he admitted. "Aunt Marge was big on church, you know, so I learned a lot of carols at church and Sunday School when I was a kid."

"I wish I knew them," Mackenzie said. "It would be fun to sing along."

"You've got your phone. Look up the words. You know the tunes, anyway."

Before long, they were belting out "Joy to the World" and laughing when each of them tripped over the verses. "How many verses are there to this song?" Declan demanded. "I only know one."

Mackenzie scrolled. "Six different verses. I can't believe your education was so limited. Only one verse. Ha!"

"Hey. You're the one that supposedly didn't know any songs."

Giggling together, they arrived on Water Street. "Where first?" Declan asked. "We can go get the tree if you like."

"Sure. Then Dakin's Hardware and keep the Save Mart for last."

"Still worried about Josiah and Estelle?"

"No. Well, maybe," she admitted. "We don't have any choice, though. We need food for Christmas dinner."

He patted her knee.

She could hardly suppress her excitement. "I hope they still have trees."

"Look here. The Lions' Club still has trees. Let's go here." She followed him over to look at the trees leaning against sawhorses.

"Looking for a tree?" A warmly wrapped man approached. "Guess you must be," he said with a grin. "Not many other reasons to be here."

Declan grinned back. "You're right. We'd like a nice one, but I know it's kind of late."

"Not too late," he said. "We did sell a lot yesterday thanks to that Sea Stars Festival, though."

Mackenzie's ears pricked up.

"That sounds good. Did you see the parade?" Declan asked, giving Mackenzie an arch glance.

"I took my grandkids, or maybe they took me," he said. "We never had a Christmas parade before in Stella Mare. It was pretty good."

"My girlfriend here was the organizer." Declan gestured toward Mackenzie.

"One of the organizers," she demurred.

"Well, good job," the man said. "I have a complaint, though."

Her stomach clenched. She'd hope the festival was really over, but she asked anyway. "Complaint?"

He grinned at her. "Well, I didn't win the giveaway."

Her shoulders relaxed. "Sorry about that," she said lightly, while Declan chuckled beside her.

"Nah, I'm just teasin'," he said. "It was a good day for the village, and everything looked pretty nice, too. Now let's find you a tree."

"I'm glad you have some left," Mackenzie said. "We are cutting it close."

"Some came in yesterday," the man said. "One of our tree farmers had some extra stock and decided to donate it to the Lions Club. Here's a really nice one." He held out a branchy evergreen.

It was squat and bushy in the lower half, but beautifully shaped on top. "That's a nice one," Mackenzie said. "Not too tall for the living room."

They quickly agreed, and the man helped Declan secure the tree in the back of the pickup. "You two have a merry Christmas there," he said.

Back in the cab of the pickup, she looked behind her to see the tree parked in the truck bed. Just like everyone else, she thought, here we are picking out our tree, taking it home to our house. A spurt of satisfaction warmed her heart.

"Dakin's next?" Declan asked. She nodded.

The hardware store was quiet on this Sunday afternoon, Charlie sipping coffee behind the counter at the back. "Hey, you!" he called out when they entered.

"Hi, Charlie," Mackenzie said. "How's business?"

He laughed. "Slow, thank goodness. Yesterday was so busy I need a slow afternoon today. Things went good, I thought."

"Yes? You think so?" She wanted to hear it again.

"Oh, yeah. No major malfunctions, right?"

She thought about Billy Seymour and the Santa suit, then slipped her hand into Declan's. "No, no major malfunctions. Thanks for being so helpful with the giveaway."

"I thought Billy was gonna be your Santa," he said, "but he must not have been because you'd never let him draw his own name."

"Santa was a mysterious stranger," Declan said.

"Right," Charlie agreed. "Very mysterious. If I heard you say 'Ho, ho, ho,' right now, I bet we could solve that mystery. But it's no never mind. Santa came to Stella Mare, Billy won the giveaway, and everything was done fair and square."

She'd never considered the fairness of the giveaway to be at issue, but Charlie said it was okay, so it had to be.

"You got a lot of folks to come to town," Charlie said. "You even got Josiah to contribute."

"Well, he contributed time and space for the food drive," Declan said drily.

"Contribution counts," Charlie said. "You did good."

"Thanks," Mackenzie said. "But now we need some decorations for our Christmas tree. What do you have left?"

The three of them picked over the lights, garland and hand-carved wooden ornaments Charlie had sourced from somewhere.

"This is our first tree," Mackenzie said.

"You two, your first year together?" Charlie looked over his glasses at her.

"That's right," Declan agreed, "but it's also her first tree ever."

"Is that right?" Charlie looked thoughtful. "You might want something special for this year. Check in at the pottery studio," he recommended. "Mrs. Innskeep might have just the thing."

"Okay," Mackenzie agreed. "Thanks, Charlie, for everything."

He looked at her over his glasses and nodded. "I'm glad you decided to stay here, Mackenzie. Not go back to Boston."

"Me?" She was so surprised her voice cracked. "I'm here for the duration."

"Good. Merry Christmas, you two."

The pottery studio yielded a ceramic starfish for the tree, as well as a little cottage dated with the year and labelled 'Our First Christmas,' personalized for them by the artist. Mackenzie listened to Declan request the words. "Mackenzie and Declan, 2018." He smiled at her and said, "The first of many."

Pleased, Mackenzie tucked the box in beside the decorations from the hardware store and put away her questions about their future. Some other time.

The final stop of the day was the Save Mart. Mackenzie's list was long, including everything on the menu for Christmas dinner. When she and Declan got to the checkout, their cart was full, and she was still ticking off items on her list.

"Well, there she is!" She looked up to see Josiah smiling – actually smiling – at her. "Getting' ready for Christmas, are ya?"

Declan spoke up. "Hi, Josiah. Still busy here?"

"Oh, yes," Josiah said. "We'll be busy right up until six p.m. on Christmas eve. Good thing you got your turkey now," he added, looking in their cart.

Mackenzie looked up as she unloaded the food onto the conveyer. "Is there a shortage?"

He laughed. "Could be. Sold a lot of turkeys yesterday. The food bank even bought some more."

"So the Sea Stars Festival worked out, did it?" Declan asked. Mackenzie glanced up sharply. Could she kick his foot and get him to stop?

"Not bad," Josiah said. "I got some ideas for next year, though."

Declan looked at Mackenzie. "Next year, eh?"

"Might be worth doin' again," Josiah opined. "Not too bad, Mackenzie." He headed through the office door.

Estelle, at the cash register, looked after him, then turned back to her work, silently sliding groceries over the scanner.

"Hi, Estelle," Mackenzie said as she followed her purchases toward the register. "Merry Christmas."

Estelle smiled, a tiny quirk of her lips, but her eyes were warm, warmer than Mackenzie had ever seen them. "Looks like you're making Christmas dinner."

"My first time," Mackenzie said. "Got any suggestions?"

The older woman kept scanning groceries, while Declan bagged them and put them back in the cart. "Looks like you got it all," she said. "You'll do fine." She pulled the last bag of carrots across the scanner.

As Mackenzie was paying and Declan started out the door with the cart, Estelle said, "Wait" and held up one finger. "I've got something for you."

She disappeared into the office and returned with a square bakery box, topped with a red bow. "Not for Christmas dinner," she said. "For today. Won't be as good on Wednesday." She handed the box to Mackenzie.

"What's in here?" she asked curiously, tugging at the tape holding it closed.

"Don't open it," Estelle warned. "It's baklava, fresh this morning from St. Stephen. For you and that man of yours."

"Estelle." Mackenzie's voice felt thick. "Thank you."

"Merry Christmas. Now go on. It's supposed to snow. Get home before the roads get slick."

Mackenzie nodded and followed Declan out the door, warmth spreading through her chest.

"Can we just eat baklava for dinner?" Mackenzie asked, looking into the box. "This looks so good."

Declan peered over her shoulder. "We probably should have something first," he said. "But I see your point. Let's get the tree up, then we can make sandwiches or something."

"Okay," she agreed. "I don't know what's involved in this tree stuff."

"I got that big tree stand from Charlie, so that's where we begin," he said. "I'll cut the bottom off the trunk outside, while you figure out where you want it to go, and then we'll get it set up. Then lights, then the other decorations."

"Okay. Clearly there is a system here," she said. "I will follow your lead."

After the tree was up and they'd hung their new decorations, Declan turned out the room lights, letting the tiny fairy lights over the pellet stove and the colours of the Christmas tree be the only illumination. Mackenzie sank into the couch. "Beautiful," she breathed. "It's magical."

Following her gaze, he sat, too. The wind whispered around the eaves in the sudden quiet.

"Now I just have to pull off Christmas dinner," she said.

"No need to stress," he said. "Dinner will be fine. I'll help."

She thought of seeing Santa in the wagon yesterday. He did know how to help.

He took her hand. "I need to talk to you about something," he said seriously.

Her stomach sank. Success as a playwright...that could mean he was ready to leave teaching. Ready to leave Stella Mare. Maybe New York hadn't been a joke. She had hoped to get through Christmas without a big upset, but she could take it. She straightened her back. "Okay."

"It was a big week," he said.

"It was," she agreed. "Your play turned out great."

He smiled. "So did your festival. But this week also cemented some things I've been thinking about."

She nodded as if she understood.

"I think I've been missing the obvious," he said. "Ignoring the evidence."

She suddenly felt shaky and weak. "Evidence for what?"

He dropped her hand and looked away. "When I step back and look at things, it seems so clear. I've always said I was a writer first, that my writing career was the main thing in my life. My novel, the one that's almost written, that's the lever for change. The play was just a fun side project."

"I understand," she said. "You want to grow your writing career."

He nodded. "I do."

She gazed at the tree again, heart sinking. "I love this tree, and I love our home. I'm so happy your play was such a success." A tear slipped down her cheek. "I finally feel like I'm settling in here."

"That's great," he said. "But why are you crying?" He touched his finger to her cheek.

"You'll be heading off, maybe at the end of the school year. Going to wherever a novelist might go. I'm happy for you, really."

"Mackenzie..."

She pushed on. "I'm happy for you, but not for me. I want you right here with me, even though I'm not being fair. I have to be honest with you."

"Mackenzie, just listen, okay?" He leaned over to look into her eyes.

"What?"

"I'm trying to tell you. All of this with the play made things clear. I'm a teacher who writes, not a writer who teaches to pay the bills."

She squinted. "Say it again, please."

He picked up her hand. "I'm a teacher. I love it, and I want to keep doing it, and yes, I still want to write, but not only that."

She felt her shoulders drop. "You want to be a teacher." How could it have taken him so long to see something so obvious to everyone else? "Chuck's dad..."

"Yeah, that was more confirmation, but honestly, I've been heading this way all year. It's just taken me a while to realize that I've already changed course, without my brain really getting it."

"That sounds dangerous," she said.

"It would be in a boat," he agreed, "but I think it's okay. It's not just the play, though."

"No?"

"It's us. You and me. This house. Our home."

She was holding her breath.

"I love this. I want to make a home here with you. I want to teach school, write books, renovate this house, hang out with you. Have friends over. Be a family."

She felt tears start. "That's what I want."

"I told you we want the same things," he said with a smile. "I was just a little slow to understand what I meant."

"I was slow to believe you," she said. "But I'm getting it now."

She curled into him as they both gazed at the tree. "How much togetherness did you have in mind?"

He tucked her head onto his shoulder. "As close as we can get."

She hesitated, then asked, "Married?" She waited to feel him pull away, but he tugged her closer.

"I was afraid to bring that up," he said. "Since you had a bad time before."

She leaned away from him so she could see his face. "That was different. A lot different." No matter how much he worked, Declan would never be like Andrew, thank goodness. "I think I'd like to be married to you."

"Duly noted," Declan said with a grin. "I might like it, too."

"It would make Josiah feel better," Mackenzie said with a giggle. She gazed at the tree, feeling him pressed against her side. Murphy stretched out on the floor in front of the pellet stove with a sigh. A gust of wind rattled the windows, but she was as cosy as she'd ever been. Home.

"Where's our little house?" Declan asked. "I don't remember hanging it up."

"Our house? Oh, yes." She got up to rummage through the bags and empty ornament boxes. "Here is it," she announced, dangling it from its green ribbon. She gazed at their names, encircled in a red heart, then looked at him. "Let's find the perfect spot."

"Not perfect. We'll find a good spot," he said. He got off the couch to hold down a branch. She slid the ribbon over the needles, and watched the tiny house swing, then settle into stability.

"Well, that's good for this Christmas," she said.

He took both her hands. "For every Christmas. Together."

Her eyes swam as she nodded. "Together."

About Annie

I write under the name Annie M. Ballard, and my women's fiction is set in the Canadian Maritimes, where I have settled after growing up in New England and living all along the East Coast of the US, plus Louisiana. The history of each place I've lived has been a part of what fuels and inspires my writing. I'm interested in how the geography and culture of places influence the people and the stories they tell about themselves.

My first book – *A Talisman of Home* – introduced Mackenzie, an American who came to the Maritimes to find the father she never knew. It's an exploration of place and the meaning of family. The Sisters of Stella Mare series is about four sisters from the same small fishing and tourist village, based on a real New Brunswick place. I capture realistic life experiences with an emphasis on how strong communities support us even in our most dire moments, and a focus on how everyday experience can be transcendent. Most of us live large lives within our own frame and that's what I want to share.

When I'm not writing, reading or thinking about writing or reading, I garden, lift barbells, bake up a storm, and play the flute (I'm a rank amateur). Sign up for my newsletter for a chat a couple of times a month, and updates on the lifting, gardening, baking and, oh yes, the writing.

Want to know more? Check out my website at https://anniemballard.com. Subscribe to my newsletter. https://www.subscribepage.com/newsfromannie

www.ingramcontent.com/pod-product-compliance
Lightning Source LLC
Chambersburg PA
CBHW030858200726
48289CB00003B/809